FICTION HOUSE PRESS
PRESENTS

MANHUNT

October 1953
Vol. 1, No. 10

This reprint edition is a facsimile of the original pulp magazine. Variations in printing and quality can be attributed to the original magazine which was printed on rough woodpulp paper. No attempt has been made to politically correct any language deemed inappropriate to the modern reader.

ISBN 978-1-64720-671-0

www.FictionHousePress.com
fictionhousepress@gmail.com

VOL. 1, NO. 10

MANHUNT

OCTOBER, 1953

CONTENTS

NOVELETTES *Page*

SHORT STORIES

FEATURES

JOHN McCLOUD, *Editor* HAL WALKER, *Managing Editor*
CHAS. W. ADAMS, *Art Director* R. E. DECKER, *Business Manager*

MANHUNT VOLUME 1, NUMBER 10, OCTOBER, 1953. Single copies 35 cents. Subscriptions, $4.00 for one year in the United States and Possessions; elsewhere $5.00 (in U. S. funds) for one year. Published monthly by Flying Eagle Publications, Inc. (an affiliate of St. John Publishing Company), 545 Fifth Avenue, New York 17, New York. Telephone MU 7-6623.

The Girl Behind the Hedge

Duncan hated Walter — so he took his revenge. He introduced Walter to a beautiful girl.

A Novelette

BY MICKEY SPILLANE

THE stocky man handed his coat and hat to the attendant and went through the foyer to the main lounge of the club. He stood in the doorway for a scant second, but in that time his eyes had seen all that was to be seen; the chess game beside the windows, the foursome at cards and the lone man at the rear of the room sipping a drink.

He crossed between the tables, nodding briefly to the card players, and went directly to the back of the room. The other man looked up from his drink with a smile. "Afternoon, inspector. Sit down. Drink?"

"Hello, Dunc. Same as you're drinking."

Almost languidly, the fellow made a motion with his hand. The waiter nodded and left. The inspector settled himself in his chair with a sigh. He was a big man, heavy without being given to fat. Only his high shoes proclaimed him for what he was. When he looked at Chester Duncan he grimaced inwardly, envying him his poise and manner, yet not willing to trade him for anything.

Here, he thought smugly, *is a man who should have everything yet has nothing. True, he has money and position, but the finest of all things, a family life, was denied him.* And with a brood of five in all stages of growth at home, the inspector felt that he had achieved his purpose in life.

The drink came and the inspector took his, sipping it gratefully. When he put it down he said, "I came to thank you for that, er . . . tip. You know, that was the first time I've ever played the market."

"Glad to do it," Duncan said. His hands played with the glass, rolling it around in his palms. His eyebrows shot up suddenly, as though he was amused at something. "I suppose you heard all the ugly rumors."

A flush reddened the inspector's face. "In an offhand way, yes. Some of them were downright ugly." He sipped his drink again and tapped a cigarette on the side table. "You know," he said, "if Walter Harrison's death hadn't been so definitely a suicide, you might be standing an investigation right now."

Duncan smiled slowly. "Come now, Inspector. The market didn't budge until after his death, you know."

"True enough. But rumor has it that you engineered it in some manner." He paused long enough to study Duncan's face. "Tell me, did you?"

"Why should I incriminate myself?"

"It's over and done with. Harrison leaped to his death from the window of a hotel room. The door was locked and there was no possible way anyone could have gotten in that room to give him a push. No, we're quite satisfied that it was suicide, and everybody that ever came in contact with Harrison agrees that he did the world a favor when he died. However, there's still some speculation about you having a hand in things."

"Tell me, Inspector, do you really think I had the courage or the brains to oppose a man like Harrison, and force him to kill himself?"

The inspector frowned, then nodded. "As a matter of fact, yes. You *did* profit by his death."

"So did *you*," Duncan laughed.

"Ummmm."

"Though it's nothing to be ashamed about," Duncan added.

"When Harrison died the financial world naturally expected that the stocks he financed were no good and tried to unload. It so happened that I was one of the few who knew they were as good as gold and bought while I could. And, of course, I passed the word on to my friends. Somebody had might as well profit by the death of a . . . a rat."

Through the haze of the smoke Inspector Early saw his face tighten around the mouth. He scowled again, leaning forward in his chair. "Duncan, we've been friends quite a while. I'm just cop enough to be curious and I'm thinking that our late Walter Harrison was cursing you just before he died."

Duncan twirled his glass around. "I've no doubt of it," he said. His eyes met the inspector's. "Would you really like to hear about it?"

"Not if it means your confessing to murder. If that has to happen I'd much rather you spoke directly to the D.A."

"Oh, it's nothing like that at all. No, not a bit, Inspector. No matter how hard they tried, they couldn't do a thing that would impair either my honor or reputation. You see, Walter Harrison went to his death through his own greediness."

The inspector settled back in his chair. The waiter came with drinks to replace the empties and the two men toasted each other silently.

"Some of this you probably know already, Inspector," Duncan said . . .

Nevertheless, I'll start at the beginning and tell you everything that happened. Walter Harrison and I met in law school. We were both young and not too studious. We had one thing in common and only one. Both of us were the products of wealthy parents who tried their best to spoil their children. Since we were the only ones who could afford certain — er — pleasures, we naturally gravitated to each other, though when I think back, even at that time, there was little true friendship involved.

It so happened that I had a flair for my studies whereas Walter didn't give a damn. At examination time, I had to carry him. It seemed like a big joke at the time, but actually I was doing all the work while he was having his fling around town. Nor was I the only one he imposed upon in such a way. Many students, impressed with having his friendship, gladly took over his papers. Walter could charm the devil himself if he had to.

And quite often he had to. Many's the time he's talked his way out of spending a week end in jail for some minor offense — and I've even seen him twist the dean around his little finger, so to speak. Oh, but I remained his loyal friend. I shared everything I had with him, including my women, and even thought it amusing when I went out on a date and met him, only to have him take my girl home.

In the last year of school the crash

came. It meant little to me because my father had seen it coming and got out with his fortune increased. Walter's father tried to stick it out and went under. He was one of the ones who killed himself that day.

Walter was quite stricken, of course. He was in a blue funk and got stinking drunk. We had quite a talk and he was for quitting school at once, but I talked him into accepting the money from me and graduating. Come to think of it, he never did pay me back that money. However, it really doesn't matter.

After we left school I went into

business with my father and took over the firm when he died. It was that same month that Walter showed up. He stopped in for a visit and wound up with a position, though at no time did he deceive me as to the real intent of his visit. He got what he came after and in a way it was a good thing for me. Walter was a shrewd businessman.

His rise in the financial world was slightly less than meteoric. He was much too astute to remain in anyone's employ for long, and with the Street talking about Harrison, the Boy Wonder of Wall Street, in every other breath, it was inevitable that he open up his own office. In a sense, we became competitors after that, but always friends.

Pardon me, Inspector, let's say that I was his friend, he never was mine. His ruthlessness was appalling at times, but even then he managed to charm his victims into accepting their lot with a smile. I for one know that he managed the market to make himself a cool million on a deal that left me gasping. More than once he almost cut the bottom out of my business, yet he was always in with a grin and a big hello the next day as if it had been only a tennis match he had won.

If you've followed his rise then you're familiar with the social side of his life. Walter cut quite a swath for himself. Twice, he was almost killed by irate husbands, and if he had been, no jury on earth would have convicted his murderer. There was the time a young girl killed herself rather than let her parents know that she had been having an affair with Walter and had been trapped. He was very generous about it. He offered her money to travel, her choice of doctors and anything she wanted . . . except his name for her child. No, he wasn't ready to give his name away then. That came a few weeks later.

I was engaged to be married at the time. Adrianne was a girl I had loved from the moment I saw her and there aren't words enough to tell how happy I was when she said she'd marry me. We spent most of our waking hours poring over plans for the future. We even selected a site for our house out on the Island and began construction. We were timing the wedding to coincide with the completion of the house and if ever I was a man living in a dream world, it was then. My happiness was complete, as was Adrianne's, or so I thought. Fortune seemed to favor me with more than one smile at the time. For some reason my own career took a sudden spurt and whatever I touched turned to gold, and in no time the Street had taken to following me rather than Walter Harrison. Without realizing it, I turned several deals that had him on his knees, though I doubt if many ever realized it. Walter would never give up the amazing front he affected.

At this point Duncan paused to study his glass, his eyes narrowing. Inspector Early remained motionless, waiting for him to go on.

"Walter came to see me," Duncan said. "It was a day I shall never forget. I had a dinner engagement with Adrianne and invited him along. Now I know that what he did was done out of sheer spite, nothing else. At first I believed that it was my fault, or hers, never giving Walter a thought . . .

Forgive me if I pass over the details lightly, Inspector. They aren't very pleasant to recall. I had to sit there and watch Adrianne captivated by this charming rat to the point where I was merely a decoration in the chair opposite her. I had to see him join us day after day, night after night, then hear the rumors that they were seeing each other without me, then discover for myself that she was in love with him.

Yes, it was quite an experience. I had the idea of killing them both, then killing myself. When I saw that that could never solve the problem I gave it up.

Adrianne came to me one night. She sat and told me how much she hated to hurt me, but she had fallen in love with Walter Harrison and wanted to marry him. What else was there to do? Naturally, I acted the part of a good loser and called off the engagement. They didn't wait long. A week later they were married and I was the laughing stock of the Street.

Perhaps time might have cured everything if things didn't turn out the way they did. It wasn't very long afterwards that I learned of a break in their marriage. Word came that Adrianne had changed and I knew for a fact that Walter was far from being true to her.

You see, now I realized the truth. Walter never loved her. He never loved anybody but himself. He married Adrianne because he wanted to hurt me more than anything else in the world. He hated me because I had something he lacked . . . happiness. It was something he searched after desperately himself and always found just out of reach.

In December of that year Adrianne took sick. She wasted away for a month and died. In the final moments she called for me, asking me to forgive her; this much I learned from a servant of hers. Walter, by the way, was enjoying himself at a party when she died. He came home for the funeral and took off immediately for a sojourn in Florida with some attractive showgirl.

God, how I hated that man! I used to dream of killing him! Do you know, if ever my mind drifted from the work I was doing I always pictured myself standing over his corpse with a knife in my hand, laughing my head off.

Every so often I would get word of Walter's various escapades, and they seemed to follow a definite pattern. I made it my business to learn more about him and before long I realized that Walter was almost frenzied in his search to find a woman he could really love. Since he was a fabulously wealthy man, he was always suspicious of a woman wanting him more than his wealth, and this very suspicion always was the thing that drove a woman away from him.

It may seem strange to you, but regardless of my attitude I saw him quite regularly. And equally strange, he never realized that I hated him so. He realized, of course, that he was far from popular in any quarter, but he never suspected me of anything else save a stupid idea of friendship. But having learned my lesson the hard way, he never got the chance to impose upon me again, though he never really had need to.

It was a curious thing, the solution I saw to my problem. It had been there all the time, I was aware of it being there, yet using the circumstance never occurred to me until the day I was sitting on my veranda reading a memo from my office manager. The note stated that Walter had pulled another coup in the market and had the Street rocking on its heels. It was one of those times when any variation in Wall Street reflected the economy of the country, and what he did was undermine the entire economic structure of the United States. It was with the greatest effort that we got back to normal without toppling, but in doing so a lot of places had to close up. Walter Harrison, however, had doubled the wealth he could never hope to spend anyway.

As I said, I was sitting there reading the note when I saw her behind the window in the house across the way. The sun was streaming in, reflecting the gold in her hair, making a picture of beauty so exquisite as to be unbelievable. A servant came and brought her a tray, and as she sat down to lunch I lost sight of her behind the hedges and the thought came to me of how simple it would all be.

I met Walter for lunch the next day. He was quite exuberant over his latest adventure, treating it like a joke.

I said, "Say, you've never been out to my place on the Island, have you?"

He laughed, and I noticed a little guilt in his eyes. "To tell the truth," he said, "I would have dropped in if you hadn't built the place for Adrianne. After all . . ."

"Don't be ridiculous, Walter. What's done is done. Look, until things get back to normal, how about staying with me a few days. You need a rest after your little deal."

"Fine, Duncan, fine! Anytime you say."

"All right, I'll pick you up tonight."

We had quite a ride out, stopping at a few places for drinks and hashing over the old days at school. At any other time I might have laughed, but all those reminiscences had taken on an unpleasant air. When we reached the house I had a few friends in to meet the fabulous Walter Harrison, left him accepting their plaudits and went to bed.

We had breakfast on the veranda. Walter ate with relish, breathing deeply of the sea air with animal-like pleasure. At exactly nine o'clock the sunlight flashed off the windows of the house behind mine as the servant threw them open to the morning breeze.

Then she was there. I waved and she waved back. Walter's head turned to look and I heard his breath catch in his throat. She was lovely, her hair a golden cascade that tumbled around her shoulders. Her blouse was a radiant white that enhanced the swell of her breasts, a gleaming contrast to the smooth tanned flesh of her shoulders.

Walter looked like a man in a dream. "Lord, she's lovely!" he said. "Who is she, Dunc?"

I sipped my coffee. "A neighbor," I said lightly.

"Do you . . . do you think I can get to meet her?"

"Perhaps. She's quite young and just a little bit shy and it would be better to have her see me with you a few times before introductions are in order."

He sounded hoarse. His face had taken on an avid, hungry look. "Anything you say, but I have to meet her." He turned around with a grin. "By golly, I'll stay here until I do, too!"

We laughed over that and went back to our cigarettes, but every so often I caught him glancing back toward the hedge with that desperate expression creasing his face.

Being familiar with her schedule, I knew that we wouldn't see her again that day, but Walter knew nothing of this. He tried to keep away from the subject, yet it persisted in coming back. Finally he said, "Incidentally, just who is she?"

"Her name is Evelyn Vaughn. Comes from quite a well-to-do-family."

"She here alone?"

"No, besides the servants she has a nurse and a doctor in attendance. She hasn't been quite well."

"Hell, she looks the picture of health."

"Oh, she is now," I agreed. I walked over and turned on the television and we watched the fights. For the sixth time a call came in for Walter, but his reply was the same. He wasn't going back to New York. I felt the anticipation in his voice, knowing why he was staying, and had to concentrate on the screen to keep from smiling.

Evelyn was there the next day and the next. Walter had taken to waving when I did and when she waved back his face seemed to light up until it looked almost boyish. The sun had tanned him nicely and he pranced around like a colt, especially when she could see him. He pestered me with questions and received evasive answers. Somehow he got the idea that his importance warranted a visit from the house across the way. When I told him that to Evelyn neither wealth nor position meant a thing he looked at me sharply to see if I was telling the truth. To have become what he was he had to be a good reader of faces and he knew that it *was* the truth beyond the shadow of a doubt.

So I sat there day after day watching Walter Harrison fall helplessly in love with a woman he hadn't met yet. He fell in love with the way she waved until each movement of her hand seemed to be for him alone. He fell in love with the luxuriant beauty of her body, letting his eyes follow her as she walked to the water from the house, aching to be close to her. She would turn sometimes and see us watching, and wave.

At night he would stand by the window not hearing what I said because he was watching her windows, hoping for just one glimpse of her, and often I would hear him repeating her name slowly, letting it roll off his tongue like a precious thing.

It couldn't go on that way. I knew it and he knew it. She had just come up from the beach and the water glistened on her skin. She laughed at something the woman said who was with her and shook her head back so that her hair flowed down her back.

Walter shouted and waved and she laughed again, waving back. The wind brought her voice to him and Walter stood there, his breath hot in my face. "Look here, Duncan, I'm going over and meet her. I can't stand this waiting. Good

Lord, what does a guy have to go through to meet a woman?"

"You've never had any trouble before, have you?"

"Never like this!" he said. "Usually they're dropping at my feet. I haven't changed, have I? There's nothing repulsive about me, is there?"

I wanted to tell the truth, but I laughed instead. "You're the same as ever. It wouldn't surprise me if she was dying to meet you, too. I can tell you this . . . she's never been outside as much as since you've been here."

His eyes lit up boyishly. "Really, Dunc. Do you think so?"

"I think so. I can assure you of this, too. If she does seem to like you it's certainly for yourself alone."

As crudely as the barb was placed, it went home. Walter never so much as glanced at me. He was lost in thought for a long time, then: "I'm going over there now, Duncan. I'm crazy about that girl. By God, I'll marry her if it's the last thing I do."

"Don't spoil it, Walter. Tomorrow, I promise you, I'll go over with you."

His eagerness was pathetic. I don't think he slept a wink that night. Long before breakfast he was waiting for me on the veranda. We ate in silence, each minute an eternity for him. He turned repeatedly to look over the hedge and I caught a flash of worry when she didn't appear.

Tight little lines had appeared at the corner of his eyes and he said, "Where is she, Dunc? She should be there by now, shouldn't she?"

"I don't know," I said. "It does seem strange. Just a moment." I rang the bell on the table and my housekeeper came to the door. "Have you seen the Vaughns, Martha?" I asked her.

She nodded sagely. "Oh, yes, sir. They left very early this morning to go back to the city."

Walter turned to me. "Hell!"

"Well, she'll be back," I assured him.

"Damn it, Dunc, that isn't the point!" He stood up and threw his napkin on the seat. "Can't you realize that I'm in love with the girl? I can't wait for her to get back!"

His face flushed with frustration. There was no anger, only the crazy hunger for the woman. I held back my smile. It happened. It happened the way I planned for it to happen. Walter Harrison had fallen so deeply in love, so truly in love that he couldn't control himself. I might have felt sorry for him at that moment if I hadn't asked him, "Walter, as I told you, I know very little about her. Supposing she is already married."

He answered my question with a nasty grimace. "Then she'll get a divorce if I have to break the guy in pieces. I'll break anything that stands in my way, Duncan. I'm going to have her if it's the last thing I do!"

He stalked off to his room. Later I heard the car roar down the road. I let myself laugh then.

I went back to New York and was there a week when my contacts told me of Walter's fruitless search. He used every means at his disposal, but he couldn't locate the girl. I gave him seven days, exactly seven days. You see, that seventh day was the anniversary of the date I introduced him to Adrianne. I'll never forget it. Wherever Walter is now, neither will he.

When I called him I was amazed at the change in his voice. He sounded weak and lost. We exchanged the usual formalities; then I said, "Walter, have you found Evelyn yet?"

He took a long time to answer. "No, she's disappeared completely."

"Oh, I wouldn't say that," I said.

He didn't get it at first. It was almost too much to hope for. "You . . . mean you know where she is?"

"Exactly."

"Where? Please, Dunc . . . where is she?" In a split second he became a vital being again. He was bursting with life and energy, demanding that I tell him.

I laughed and told him to let me get a word in and I would. The silence was ominous then. "She's not very far from here, Walter, in a small hotel right off Fifth Avenue." I gave him the address and had hardly finished when I heard his phone slam against the desk. He was in such a hurry he hadn't bothered to hang up. . . .

Duncan stopped and drained his glass, then stared at it remorsefully. The Inspector coughed lightly to attract his attention, his curiosity prompting him to speak. "He found her?" he asked eagerly.

"Oh yes, he found her. He burst right in over all protests, expecting to sweep her off her feet."

This time the Inspector fidgeted nervously. "Well, go on."

Duncan motioned for the waiter and lifted a fresh glass in a toast. The Inspector did the same. Duncan smiled gently. "When she saw him she laughed and waved. Walter Harrison died an hour later . . . from a window in the same hotel."

It was too much for the Inspector. He leaned forward in his chair, his forehead knotted in a frown. "But what happened? Who was she? Damn it, Duncan . . ."

Duncan took a deep breath, then gulped the drink down.

"Evelyn Vaughn was a hopeless imbecile," he said.

"She had the beauty of a goddess and the mentality of a two-year-old. They kept her well tended and dressed so she wouldn't be an object of curiosity. But the only habit she ever learned was to wave bye-bye. . . ."

Squeeze Play

A Shell Scott Story

BY RICHARD S. PRATHER

Pretty Willis was vain about his looks. Spoil them, and you'd be dead. So Scott hit Willis in the face with a gun.

PRETTY Willis was a killer as proud of his appearance as of his gun, and he had no use for private detectives unless he was hitting them over the head. Consequently he had no use at all for one Shell Scott. But at four o'clock Tuesday afternoon he barged into my office in the Hamilton Building and said flatly, "Get your coat, Scott. You're leaving." It was an order.

I was watching guppies in the aquarium on top of my bookcase, so all I knew at first was that there was a nasty-voiced slob behind me. But I turned around, recognized him and said, "The hell you say. Bag your lip, Pretty."

His handsome face flushed. "You know who I am. You know better than to spring with a crack like that."

To Pretty both statements meant the same thing: If you knew who he was, you talked softly to him. We'd never met before, socially or unsocially, but I knew a lot of things about him and all of them except his appearance were nauseating.

He was handsome enough in a tortured sort of way. He stood almost my height, six-two, but I had twenty-five pounds over his one-eighty — not counting the gun which would be under his coat. Besides the gun and his weight-lifter's build, he had porcelain caps on his teeth, jet-black hair the precise color of Tintair number fourteen, and carefully manicured, too-shiny nails. His eyebrows were dark and neat, the space between them plucked as bare and empty as I imagined his mind was. Pretty Willis was possibly the vainest man in Los Angeles — but also one of the toughest. He'd been in a number of brawls, and was still pretty only because he could take care of himself.

He said deliberately, "Snap it up. Hackman wants to see you. We hear you been looking for Leroy Crane."

He was right. Mrs. Leroy Crane had been my client for about twenty-four hours now. She wanted me to find her husband — or, perhaps, late husband. Leroy was four days late. He worked — or had worked — as Hackman's accountant, so I figured Leroy was already starting to decompose.

Hackman was Wallace Hackman, Crook in capitals, with his fat fingers in everything from dope to sudden death. He was not only ruthless but stupid, and would never have got as high in the rackets as he had except for one thing: he didn't trust any man alive. He wouldn't give you the correct time if he could help it, and he didn't even trust his right-hand man, Pretty Willis, behind his back. His complicated little hierarchy was a lot like a communist club: crooks watching crooks who in turn watched other crooks, and all reporting to the top, Hackman.

Complicated, maybe, but as a result nobody had ever got enough on Hackman to haul him into court, much less put him behind bars. His previous accountant, who by the nature of his work would naturally have learned more than anybody else about the boss' business, had simply disappeared a couple years back — after which Leroy Crane got the well-paid, unhealthy job. It seemed likely that Hackman wouldn't want me to find Leroy.

Pretty Willis said, "Get a move on. Hack don't like to wait. And don't give me no more lip."

"You run along and pluck your eyebrows, Pretty," I said. "Tell your boss I'll see him when and if I get time." I wasn't exactly dying to see Hackman because a lot of times seeing Hackman and dying were practically the same thing.

Pretty walked up in front of me, stopped, started to say something and then strangled it in his throat.

It's funny, but I wasn't thinking about much of anything except the best way to tie him up. I knew Pretty was handy with his hands — and feet and knees for that matter — but even if that was part of his business, it was also part of mine and had been from my Marine days down to here. I just wanted to be careful that I didn't mark him up. He would be mad enough at me for simply clobbering him, but there was no point in driving him insane. His face was to him what soft lingerie or French postcards are to some other guys; it was his fetish; he was in love with it. If I mashed his face, he'd kill me when he could, if he could. Actually, the best way to handle Pretty was with a gun, and I glanced toward my desk where the .38 Colt Special and harness were draped over my coat.

I learned one thing for sure: You should never take your eyes off a guy like Pretty. While I was looking toward my gun, he knocked me down. I'd expected him to chat a bit more, but I had hurt his feelings so he just hauled off and caught me not only off guard, but behind the ear. I landed on my fanny, more surprised to be down there on the floor than hurt, and I was too surprised for too long.

Pretty swung his leg forward and the pointed toe of his shoe went into my stomach like a meal. It caught me in the solar plexus and I bent forward, grabbing for his leg, my sight blurring as tiny red and black spots danced in the air around me, and I got a grip on his foot and twisted. I did all of it just like the book says, but the book didn't say what happened when you were dizzy, paralyzed, and couldn't twist a wet noodle.

But I found out. I knew Pretty was way up there above me, that he'd be swinging his gun down toward my head, but it was like knowing the earth is moving; I couldn't do a thing to stop it. . . .

When I came to I was on a soft couch, though I didn't realize even that at first. My head ached, and I couldn't remember what had happened or why my head should be throbbing. I felt my skull and found a large bump. There was a clue. Then I remembered and opened my eyes. A few feet from me, in an overstuffed chair large enough to hold his overstuffed bulk, was Hackman. That meant I must be in his suite on the top floor of L.A.'s new Hotel Statler.

"Hello, Hackman," I said. "Hello, you sonofabitch."

He chuckled. A lot of the top racket boys are pleasant, personable men, but not this oily, pudgy, baby-faced and round-bellied slug. I shut my eyes and shook my head to clear fog from my brain. I knew Hackman would want to talk about Leroy Crane, and I thought back to what Crane's wife had told me.

Yesterday Ann Crane, a cute little wide-eyed doll, had phoned me and I'd gone to see her. She'd cried and told me that three nights before, husband Leroy had phoned her and said he wouldn't see her for a few days. He had a big deal cooking and would make up for the separation — their first — with mink coats and diamonds. She hadn't heard from him since.

She'd convinced me not only that she had no idea what he'd been talking about, but that she was ready to crack up. I got a photograph of thin-faced, rather homely Leroy, learned all I could about him, including what his job was with Hackman, and through it all were her tears. Tears out of brown eyes, trailing down over soft cheeks, glistening on curved red lips.

After reaching agreement about my fee I'd gone back to the office and put my lines out, let it be known in the right places that I was looking for Leroy. And then in had walked Pretty Willis.

I opened my eyes and said, "Get it off your chest, Hackman."

He glanced toward the door. "Wait outside, boys."

The "boys" were Pretty Willis and a little hood named Shadow who was so skinny and dishonest that he always weighed himself with his gun on. He must have helped Pretty lug me up here. When I saw Pretty, anger exploded inside me and I got to my feet, wobbling a bit. But before I could take a step toward him both men had gone out the door and closed it. I started after them but Hackman said, "Sit down. All I gotta do is grunt and you've had it."

I told him to shut up, but I sat down. He was right. If I'd had a gun, though, he might have been wrong. Hackman wheezed and jiggled, shifting from one monstrous buttock to the other, then he said, "Scott, I know you don't like me. And I got no love for you, neither. But we don't have to like each other to cooperate."

"Get to the point."

"I want Crane myself. In case you get to him before me, I want him, see? I can make it worth your while."

"Nuts. I wouldn't give you a drink in the desert. I wouldn't even give you conversation if you hadn't asked me so politely." I went on from there. I watched him get angry, watched his oily face shade from white into pink, and when I finished he knew for sure I wasn't going to give him a damned thing except trouble.

Suddenly he said, "Shut your face, Scott. And blow. Blow fast before you start leaking someplace besides your mouth." He leaned forward and said, "But understand this, Scott. I want Crane myself. And I mean to get him. You get in my way an inch, move one inch out of line, and I'll see that you get dead."

Some of the hot anger drained out of me because it finally had occurred to me that this was a strange conversation we were having if Leroy Crane were alive. And if

Hackman was still looking for him, he almost surely *was* alive.

I thought about that for a moment, then said slowly, "So that's it. Crane powdered and now you're sweating."

In his own cute way he told me I was constipated. Then he went on, "You drop it. Stop looking for Crane. Forget you ever heard of him." He didn't make any more specific threats, but his voice was lower and the words came out like ice cubes. I started to say something else but Hackman said, "Get out," then raised his voice and shouted, "Pretty!"

Pretty Willis came inside followed by Shadow. There weren't any guns in sight, but I knew there would be if I wiggled. Hackman said, "Beat it, Scott. Don't forget nothing I told you."

I walked to the door and as I passed the two thugs I said pointedly, "Be seeing you, Pretty." He showed me his too-white teeth and chuckled, "I'm panicked." He and Shadow followed me to the outer door. Shadow opened it and I went through, then started to turn around for a last word. I didn't make it. While Pretty was behind me he must have taken his gun out. I assume that's what he slammed against the back of my skull.

I stumbled forward, fell to my hands and knees and there was barely enough strength in my arms to hold me up off the floor. Laughter grated behind me. I guess it took me about a minute to get to my feet and turn around, and by that time I was alone with my insanity. I left, went back to the office, found my gun still there and strapped it on, and returned to the Statler lobby before even a semblance of reason returned.

Half a dozen of Hackman's boys were scattered around in the chairs and divans. One of them stood up and the rest looked at me, grinning. There wasn't a thing I could do about it. I had been knocked down, kicked, threatened and sapped, and if I wanted to keep on living I had to take it — at least for a while longer.

But from then on I stopped sleeping except for short naps in my Cad or slumped over my office desk. I didn't go near my apartment. I looked for Leroy Crane. Every ex-con, every tipster and stoolie I'd ever had anything to do with got word one way or another from me that they could name their price if they gave me a lead to Crane. I saw Ann again, told her that her husband was at least alive, and that I'd find him, but I learned nothing new from her except that she was the cryingest babe I had ever seen. I kept my eyes peeled for any of Hackman's pals, and I looked for Pretty as hard as I looked for Leroy. For two long days nothing happened.

On Thursday afternoon my office phone rang and a woman's soft, lilting voice said, "Mr. Scott? I can take you to Leroy Crane. For a hundred dollars."

"You just made a hundred. Where and when?"

"Right now in room sixteen, Porter Hotel on L.A. Street."

"Is Crane there?"

"No, stupid. I am. Bring the C-note. Incidentally, my name's Billie."

I hung up and glared at the phone. Billie could be on the level, and probably was, but I didn't like it. A hundred dollars didn't seem like much payment for her information.

It was one of those mangy hotels on Los Angeles Street a block from Main. On the wrong side of Main. Somebody had thrown up in the narrow entrance at street level; worn wooden stairs shuddered as I walked up them into a dimly-lighted hallway that smelled like dead mice. The door of room sixteen looked as if it would turn into powder and termites if I knocked hard on it, so I tapped gently with my left hand, right hand curled around the .38's butt in my coat pocket. The door opened and I stared.

This was almost like getting kicked in the stomach again. It would be impossible to describe her exactly because there aren't any three-dimensional words, but she looked so warm and wild and wonderful that my mouth went down and then up like a small slow elevator while I listened to a voice like a breeze saying, "Come on in. I'm Billie. You bring the money?"

"Yeah. Hello. Yeah. I brought the money. Uh . . ."

The "Uh . . ." was because Billie wasn't wearing much of anything. She had on a robe which reached nearly to the floor and covered every inch of skin from the neck down, but it was thin enough to suit me, and that is pretty goddamned thin. She held the robe together with both hands — there was so much to cover that it took both hands — and stepped aside as I walked in.

I glanced around to make sure we were alone, then turned to look at the gal again. She was tall, with white skin as smooth as smoke, with mist-gray eyes, with long black hair and pleasantly full lips and things. She let me look, even seemed to help me a little, and I asked her, "Where do we go from here?"

"Nowhere if you don't have the hundred. Hand it over and I'll take you to Crane."

"Not in that outfit." I took two fifty-dollar bills from my pocket.

She laughed, walked past me and flopped on a rickety bed, plucking the two fifties from my hand as she went by. I was just starting to wonder what such a choice, expensive-looking tomato was doing in this dump, and where she thought she was going in that robe and nothing else, and I might have saved myself some trouble if I'd continued thinking like that. Only right then was when she flopped on the bed.

I'm sure she hadn't planned it

quite the way it happened, because the bed springs broke. There was a great deal of activity for about two seconds there, and that was long enough for the guy to come up behind me. I hadn't been worried about anybody getting behind me because only the gal and I had been in the room and there weren't any adjoining doors — just the front door. Just the one I had my back to. Maybe I should have worried about that door behind me, considering what a phony deal this now seemed to be, but I was stupid. And if you were staring open-mouthed at a babe flying through the air with arms and legs waving at you, and bouncing to the sound of twanging springs, and no longer clutching a robe which had been thin enough to begin with, you, too, would be stupid.

But what tipped me was that the gal was paying no attention to either my face or her nudity, but was looking at a spot past my left shoulder. And maybe I heard something. I don't know now. I just know I ducked and dropped as the blow fell, and something jarred against my skull, glancing off and not getting me squarely enough to knock me out. It hurt, and it dazed me, but I still had enough sense left to reach behind me as I went down, get one hand on a trousers-covered leg and yank.

The leg slipped out of my hand as the guy fell, but I flipped over in time to see him sprawling on his back. He rolled over and jumped up again as I got my feet under me and stood up straight. It was Pretty Willis. I should have known. Every time a guy came up behind me and batted me it was Pretty Willis. Only this time I was facing him, looking at him.

The sap he'd used was on the floor, and he didn't have a gun in his hand — but he dug under his coat for one and I jumped for him. I slammed into him and my weight jarred him back against the wall as I drove my right fist forward, knuckles projecting to dig into the soft spot in his belly. Somehow his elbow got in the way, and then the hard heel of his other hand crashed under my chin, snapping my head back. I staggered slightly but in the same moment I sliced my right hand up in a tight arc, felt its edge crack against the bony structure of his face. I caught my balance, turned toward him and saw a trickle of blood under his nose, his lips pulled back tight over white teeth. He swung a hand at me and when I jerked my head aside his other fist came out of nowhere and exploded against my chin.

At least he hit me so hard that it felt like an explosion. All the colors in the room blended into a shimmering gray for a moment as I fell backwards. The floor thudded against my back. Then my vision cleared enough so I could see Pretty still bent over from the force of his swing, see him straighten up and leap toward me.

While I wasn't in the best shape of my life I could have rolled out of the way. But I didn't. I didn't even start to. Pretty had already started to dive toward me, hands extended, before I jerked my legs up off the floor and toward my chest, thinking even as I did it about the hell this bastard had given me. Then I drove my legs forward and my feet burst through his outstretched hands as if they were paper; my hard leather heels jarred into his face; and Pretty wasn't pretty any more. His body jerked, hung for a moment in the air, then dropped limply to the floor. Red stain flowed from his cheek, covered exposed white bone, seeped into the carpet.

I glanced over my shoulder at the girl, who was still on the bed, then I felt Pretty's neck to see if it was broken. It wasn't. I'll never know why it wasn't. I got up, walked to the bed and stood over Billie. She licked her lips, swallowed, stared up at me.

"Spill it," I sa'd.

She shook her head, said nothing. I bunched her black hair in one hand. "Give me some straight answers or wind up like him. Take your pick, beautiful."

She bit her lips but didn't answer. Then she looked at Pretty. He lay on his back, face toward us. I knew I couldn't slug Billie around, but the expression of fright on her face gave way slowly to revulsion, and that gave me an idea.

I grabbed her, pulled her off the bed and twisted her arms behind her, then shoved her across the room, forced her to kneel by the unconscious man. She struggled to get away but I held her firmly and pressed her face closer and closer to his. When I let her go there was a smudge of blood on her cheek. She wiped it off, stared at her stained fingers, then spoke, trying to keep the sickness out of her voice, keep from actually becoming sick.

I was lucky to be talking to Billie because Hackman hadn't trusted even Pretty with the details I wanted to hear. But she knew it all — Billie was Hackman's woman. And she told me all of it. Leroy Crane had found out that Hackman had ordered the death of his previous accountant when said accountant learned too much about the boss. For more than a year now, Crane had kept a detailed record of every financial move Hackman had made — including taxes Hackman had paid and what he *should* have paid. Crane had originally started preserving his info as a guarantee of his own safety when and if Hackman decided that accountant Crane, too, had to go. It had started out like that but had turned into the old squeeze play, a shakedown.

Crane, with his typed information supported by a mass of documents and figures, had phoned Hackman — on that night when Crane hadn't showed up at home — and told Hackman he could have the file of information for a cool half million;

otherwise Crane would turn the dope over to the income-tax boys and settle for the "informer's fee," the informant's share of delinquent taxes collected — while Hackman would wind up in the federal clink. After telling Hackman he would phone again in a week, Crane had hung up.

So Hackman had to get those papers, even if he had to pay a half-million dollars for them. But now he was trying to find Crane and work him over, beat the location of the papers out of him, then put a bullet into his brain. Crane, knowing what would happen to him if he were found, had dropped completely out of sight.

I asked Billie why Pretty had jumped me and she kept talking. "Hack knows now that you've been seeing a lot of Mrs. Crane..He didn't know that at first. This is too important for him to take any chance of a slip when he grabs her. So he had to make sure you were out of—"

"When he what? *Grabs* her?"

"Crane has the papers, but maybe he thinks more of his wife than he does of a half-million dollars." The trace of a smile curved her smooth lips as she said, "Crane must have thought nobody would bother his wife, at least not when he had all that stuff on the boss. But Crane was wrong if he did."

"When?" I said. "When are they —"

That slight smile again stopped me. "Oh," she said slowly, "they probably have her by now."

I turned and ran for the door, jumping over Pretty. I was clear down on the street and in my Cad before I thought of what it meant to leave him back there, unconscious but soon to be awake — and looking at his face. He was a little psycho anyway, and now he'd go off the deep end, crazy mad. He'd do his damndest to kill me, but there wasn't time to go back. There wasn't time for anything but Ann.

There wasn't even time for Ann. When I reached her home she was gone. The door was ajar and a wrinkled carpet, a tipped-over end table were mute signs of a struggle.

It was four o'clock Thursday afternoon. On Friday afternoon, at three o'clock, the party started coming to a head. I spent those intervening twenty-three hours without sleep, and I did everything I could to find Ann or Leroy, with no success. I looked for Pretty and Billie but didn't find them; I did find Hackman holed up in the Statler with half a dozen thugs around him, and not being suicidal I left him alone. There was one way left, and it was all I had so I took it.

For six hours now I'd been parked near the Statler where I could watch the exits. From what I knew of Hackman I was sure of one thing: he would, one way or another, get his hands on Crane's file of papers, but Hackman would also make sure they were his *own* hands. The only man alive with information which could put Hackman in prison was Crane. If Hackman let one of his underlings pick up the papers, that underling would then have in his hands enough to put the boss in jail or else squeeze him dry — and there was a very good chance the other boys around Hackman would squeeze a lot harder than Crane. I knew Hackman wouldn't trust any of his hoodlums with his right name if he could avoid it; he sure as hell wouldn't hand them the end of the noose around his neck. At least that's the way I had it figured; that was what I was counting on. If I kept my eye on Hackman, didn't lose him, I'd be in at the finish.

At three P.M., it started. Pretty Willis arrived.

He parked in a no-parking zone and ran into the hotel. I almost missed him, because I was watching for any sign of Hackman, and I would have missed Pretty if it hadn't been for his face. It was swathed in white bandages and he looked like something out of a horror picture as he ran limping across the sidewalk. Two minutes later Pretty came out — with Hackman. They drove away and I tailed them to Forty-Sixth Street, to a rooming house. They went inside, came back to their car with Shadow, the skinny hood. And with Ann. They drove to Broadway and I followed, keeping a car between them and me and the farther they went the more puzzled I got. Shadow drove through the business district, turned right beyond First, swung back into Main and parked squarely in front of the City Hall. I didn't get it, but I double-parked a few yards behind them, taking a chance they'd spot me, because whatever was happening, I wanted to be close. Shadow stayed in the car with Ann; Pretty and Hackman got out and started walking up the stone steps of the Main Street entrance of City Hall. And then it made sense.

Standing between high cement columns before the huge entrance was Leroy Crane, tall and thin, thin-faced, haggard, with a leather briefcase in one hand. He looked past the two men, toward the car, toward Ann. At the top of the steps the three men talked, argued; Crane shook his head, pointed toward the car.

It was clear enough now. Hackman was trading Leroy's wife for the stuff in the briefcase, getting the noose off his neck without spending a buck — and Leroy was the guy in the squeeze now. But Leroy was playing it smart. He was going to make the trade, but not in a place where he could be shot in the back. Behind Crane in the City Hall lobby was a guard, a cop was standing halfway down the block, in the building were everything from the Mayor to office workers to firemen to hundreds of policemen.

After some more argument Hackman turned and waved to Shadow.

He and the girl got out of the car. Ann walked a few feet away, looking all the time at her husband. I got out of the Cad, grabbed my gun and started walking toward them, tightness swelling in my chest, stomach knotting. For a moment their figures were still, as if frozen. There seemed no movement at all and none of them had yet seen me. Then Hackman took the briefcase from Crane, looked inside and pawed briefly through its contents, shut it and gripped it tightly as he and Pretty started down the steps. Shadow walked rapidly toward the car and Ann started running toward the big entrance and her husband.

It was as if a rigid tableau had dissolved into separate lines of movement, except for the still figure of Crane, standing motionless and looking toward Ann. And then came the explosion; then it happened; then Main Street blew up in our faces.

Hackman spotted me.

He stopped, reached out and clutched Pretty's arm. From twenty feet away and below him on the sidewalk I could see his fat, oily face get white. Pretty turned his bandaged head and stared at me, his eyes wide above the strips of gauze and tape. Hackman's mouth stretched open and he thrust both hands toward me, pulling his head into his neck, fat cheeks jiggling. But not Pretty, not that crazy bastard. All the hate boiled up in Pretty and overflowed when he saw me, and his mashed face twitched beneath the bandgages as his hand went under his coat.

I yelled at him, told him to stop, but he didn't hear me or just plain didn't give a damn. I even let him get the gun in his hand, bring it out from under his coat, but when sunlight gleamed on the .45's rapidly swinging barrel, there wasn't any choice for me.

The first slug from my .38 caught him high on the chest and I squeezed the trigger again as he staggered just enough so my second shot missed him and the slug caromed off one of the high cement columns fronting City Hall. Pretty convulsively triggered his .45, but by then the gun was pointing down at the sidewalk. I heard the bullet crack viciously against the walk and whine away as I fired the third shot from my Colt. It was the last shot, too, because it caught him in the throat and sliced the jugular cleanly.

You've got to see something like that to believe it. You wouldn't think the red fountain of a man's blood would squirt so far through the air, leave such a long, wide, snakelike stream against the cement, a stream that spread wider and uglier even as Pretty fell into it. He hit the cement with his side, rolled over onto his face and sprawled across two of the steps, awkward, puppetlike, very messily dead.

I thought a slug had caught Hackman, because he stumbled and fell down the steps quivering like a life-size mound of Jello, but from the corner of my eye I saw him reach bottom squirming, face down, hands wrapped around the top of his head. He was just scared, sweating plasma.

And then there was nothing but cops.

They came from everywhere except out of the sky. There were uniformed cops, plainclothes cops, cops from Robbery and Homicide and Forgery and Christ knows what. There were cops milling about, and possibly jumping up and down, and sirens and squad cars converging, and this was for sure the goddamnedest commotion ever seen on lower Main Street. Well, what can you expect when you start shooting up City Hall?

Somewhere in there a policeman on my right raised a gun toward me and I swung around yelling as he fired. The slug went past me and I looked over my shoulder to see Shadow, a red stain on his chest, gun falling from his hand and clanking against the sidewalk just before Shadow fell too. There was a blurred glimpse of Ann clinging to Leroy on one of the middle steps, of uniforms, of shouting red faces; and one guy with halitosis got his face close to mine and swore at me, and I swore.

It might have been a minute or it might have been ten, but then the landscape sighed and settled, people stopped milling, Main Street settled down. There was much jawing and yakking and explaining, and cops looked at the papers in Leroy's briefcase and beamed happily; and there was weeping because naturally Ann was bawling away as usual, only this time it was different.

And everybody was hauled away, including me for an hour after which somebody patted me on the back and told me to get some sleep. I got in a word with Ann, alone now because her husband was in a cell, and I told her Leroy wouldn't get off scot-free but it shouldn't be bad, and she cried and thanked me.

I went out of City Hall free as a bird and walked to my car. A man was mopping up red stain from the big cement steps. I headed for home, for sleep, and on the way I thought about the case, about Hackman. He'd given me a lot of trouble, but now that it was over I actually felt sorry for him. Where he was going he'd want a lot of things, miss a lot of things — but, God, how he was going to miss Billie.

But, then, she was a woman almost any man would miss. And I remembered her standing in the doorway, mist-gray eyes in her soft white face, a voice like whispering winds, a shape . . . a shape . . .

Come to think of it, she still owed me a hundred bucks.

BY

RICHARD DEMING

He hadn't even touched the girl. But there was no way in the world he could prove it . . .

Balanced Account

When the doorbell rang, Gerald Mason laid aside his book and glanced at the mantel clock in surprise. Eleven thirty P.M. was an odd time for callers.

Without haste he rose from his easy chair and crossed the front room to the door, a tall, leanly muscled man with the coordinated movements of an athlete. The man at the front door was a thin, poker-faced individual in his thirties.

To Mason's inquiring look he said, "You Gerald Mason?"

"Yes."

The thin man exhibited a small silver shield. "I'm Detective Harry Sullivan, Mr. Mason. I have a warrant for your arrest."

As Mason stepped back with his mouth open, the detective moved past him into the front room.

"What are you talking about?" Mason asked. "I haven't done anything."

"The warrant is for criminal attack, Mr. Mason. Better get a coat on."

"Criminal attack!" Mason repeated incredulously. "You mean rape?"

Detective Sullivan looked at him expressionlessly. "We book it under the polite term, 'criminal attack.' Get a move on, Mr. Mason. I haven't got too much patience with people like you."

"But this is absurd, officer. You've made some kind of mistake."

"If it's a mistake, we'll straighten it out downtown, Mr. Mason. I said get your coat on. Unless you'd rather go in shirt sleeves." Removing handcuffs from his pocket, the detective jingled them expectantly and regarded Mason with cold eyes.

Mason stared from the handcuffs to the man's expressionless face, then turned toward the stairway. Sullivan followed a step behind him, up the stairs, down a hall and into a bedroom. He watched silently as Mason knotted a tie and shrugged on a suit coat.

While he waited, the detective's glance roved about the room and finally stopped on a photograph atop the chiffonier. Idly he walked over to examine it, discovering it was the likeness of an attractive woman of about thirty.

"Your wife, Mr. Mason?" he asked.

"Yes."

The detective looked him over. "She'll be damn proud of you."

"She's been dead for two years," Mason said shortly. "May I phone a lawyer before we go?"

"You'll be given opportunity to do that after you're booked," the detective said.

At police headquarters the fat desk lieutenant looked Mason over with the same contempt Detective Harry Sullivan had made no effort to conceal.

"Full name?" he asked.

"Gerald M. Mason. Lieutenant, what is this all about?"

The lieutenant wrote the name in his log book. "You'll know in a minute, Mr. Mason. Address?"

"Twenty-four Park Plaza. Lieutenant, I want to know what I'm charged with."

The desk lieutenant wrote down the address before looking up. Then he stared straight into Mason's face and said, "Even rapists get their full constitutional rights down here, Mr. Mason. But until you're booked, just answer questions and otherwise keep your mouth shut. I haven't got much use for sex criminals." Lowering his eyes again, he said, "Age?"

Mason glared down at the man without answering until the lieutenant looked up impatiently. Then he said in a strangled voice, "Thirty-four."

"Occupation?"

"Professional football coach. I coach the White Rams."

The lieutenant looked startled. Raising his eyes again, he said, "Oh, *that* Gerald Mason. I saw the game that made you All American thirteen years ago." To Detective Sullivan, who was standing quietly to one side, he remarked, "Don't some of the damnedest people do these things, Harry?"

Sullivan merely shrugged. Completing his entries, the lieutenant closed his log book.

"May I phone a lawyer now?" Mason asked in a tight voice.

"In a few minutes," Detective Sullivan said. "First I want you to meet some people."

He led Mason into a room which, apparently, was normally employed as the showup room, for it was long and narrow and had a stage at its far end. On the steps of the stage sat a man and a girl, but both rose when the detective and Mason entered. Mason knew them both. The man, Wendell Simms, was his next-door neighbor and the girl was Simms's daughter, Patricia Ann.

Patricia Ann's body had developed into that of a woman before she managed fully to outgrow the appealing awkwardness of adolescence. Full bosomed, with softly padded hips and rounded legs, she gave an impression of physical maturity until she moved. But motion gave away her youth, for she had not entirely conquered the gangling coltishness of the teen-ager.

At the moment fright made her movements more jerkily adolescent than ever.

As always when he saw Patricia Ann, Mason had to brake his thoughts with the stern warning that he was nearly twice the girl's age. She was so ripe, so defenseless and so ready for plucking, it was an effort to remind himself that she was little more than a child, and the necessity for making the effort always flooded him with guilt. Now he grew conscious of the detective's sharp gaze studying his reaction, and was unable to prevent himself from flushing.

Patricia Ann's father was tall and thin-lipped and middle aged, and his expression at the moment was that of an avenging preacher. As he strode the length of the narrow room, his eyes fixed burningly on Mason's face, the girl had to maintain a sort of stumbling run to keep up. When the detective prevented what looked like an intended physical attack on Mason by stepping in front of him and placing a hand on Wendell Simms' chest, the girl cowered half behind her father, her eyes wide and frightened.

"Take it easy, Mr. Simms," Sullivan advised. "I know how you feel. I've got a couple of daughters myself. But the law is capable of taking care of rapists."

"What the hell is this all about, Simms?" Mason asked.

His neighbor peered at him with hate, but when the detective cautiously moved aside, he made no further attempt at assault. "You stinking punk!" he said. "She's not even eighteen!"

Mason looked at him in amazement. "Are you under the impression I did anything to Patricia Ann?"

The detective cut in with, "If you don't mind, I'll ask the questions." He looked at Patricia Ann. "All right, Miss. Is this the man who attacked you?"

The girl's terrified eyes flicked at Mason, immediately moved away and centered on a spot on the floor. Her lips moved, but when no sound came, she merely nodded her head. Angrily Mason started to open his mouth, but at a sharp glance from the detective, he decided to subside until he heard the full details of this fantastic charge.

"Was this forcible, Miss?" the detective asked. "Did you resist him?"

"Of course she resisted him," Simms snapped.

Sullivan said in a definite tone, "Let the young lady answer, Mr. Simms. It's at least statutory rape in any event, since she's a month under eighteen. But the difference between statutory rape and rape with force is about fifteen years in the pen. We have to be sure." Again he looked at the girl. "Well, Miss?"

Her face worked with a mixture of shame and fright. Avoiding Mason's gaze, she glanced at her father with an almost cringing expression. Then she said huskily, "Yes, I tried to fight him off. He forced me."

Now past the stage where anything could astonish him, Mason examined the girl's face with a kind of exasperated curiosity. But she refused to look back at him.

The detective said, "I'd like you to tell me exactly what happened, Miss."

"I . . . Do I have to talk about it? Can't we . . . can't we just let it go?"

"And let this rapist continue to walk the streets?" her father said.

In a tone of weary patience Sullivan said, "Mr. Simms, if you're going to insist on butting in, we may as well have your story first. Go ahead and tell it."

Wendell Simms glared at Mason. "I caught him right in the act, officer. He had Pat on the ground between our two garages, and when he heard me call out, he jumped up and ran into his house. After I asked Pat if she was hurt and she said she wasn't, I ran after him. But he had locked the doors and refused to answer."

Mason's reaction to the girl's charge had been primarily one of indignant anger unmixed with any great concern, for he assumed that for some incomprehensible reason she had simply made up the story of attack and convinced her father of it. Until this moment he felt he would have no great difficulty in convincing both her father and the police that she was lying. But in the face of the elder Simms's testimony that he actually witnessed the attack, a sudden chill of apprehension ran along Mason's spine.

"When was this supposed to have taken place?" he asked.

When Simms only continued to glare at him, the detective answered the question. "About ten o'clock, according to his original complaint." He glanced at his watch. "Just short of two hours ago."

"Then whoever Simms saw with his daughter couldn't have been me. I was out in the middle of the lake fishing from eight thirty to nearly eleven. I hadn't been back in the house twenty minutes when you rang the doorbell."

"Were you with anyone?" Sullivan asked.

Mason shook his head. "I went out alone."

"Maybe you can show me the fish you caught."

"They weren't biting tonight." Then Mason said hopefully, "My line would still be wet. That ought to prove I'm telling the truth."

"Or that you prepared an alibi by dunking it in the bathtub. Go on, Mr. Simms. Start right at the beginning and tell me everything."

Simms took a deep breath and began to speak in an obviously restrained voice. Mason, recognizing the hopelessness of protest at this particular moment, made no further interruption.

"As I told you, it was about ten o'clock," Simms said. "Pat was supposed to be over at a friend's house studying for a high-school exam. Young Judy Merritt, down at the end of our block and across the street. I was carrying out the garbage for my wife, and since it was quite dark, I moved rather carefully along the back walk. I suppose that's why Mason didn't hear me coming. Just as I got even with the garage, I heard a woman let out a sort of gasping moan.

"I went over to the corner of the garage and peered in the direction from which the sound came. I saw them on the ground not fifteen feet away, but in the darkness they were just dim shapes. I could see clearly enough to tell what was going on, but not well enough to tell who it was. It never even occurred to me the girl might be Pat. I just assumed a pair of lovers were using my back yard, and the idea irked me. I called out, 'Hey! What's going on here?'

"Instantly the man jumped up and ran toward the rear of Mason's house. Then the girl got up. My eyes were now beginning to adjust to the darkness, and also I had stepped closer after the man ran off, and I was shocked to discover the girl was my daughter. She started to cry, but I stopped her from becoming hysterical by slapping her face. Then I asked her if the man who had run away was Mason and she said yes."

The detective interrupted. "If you couldn't recognize the man in the dark, how'd you happen to ask that?"

In a tone of rigid self-control, as though he felt the slightest relaxation might send him into a frothing rage, Simms said, "He ran into Mason's house."

"You actually saw him enter?"

"It was too dark for that. But he was running directly toward the rear door when he disappeared in the darkness. Besides, there isn't any question about his identity. Pat certainly knows who attacked her."

"All right. Go on."

"I asked Pat if she was hurt, and she said she didn't think so. I told her to go inside and then I went over to pound on Mason's back door. When he didn't answer, I tried the door, but it was locked. I tried the front door too, but it was locked also. I could see a light in the front room and I think that's where he was, but I couldn't see in because the drapes were drawn. Finally I gave up trying to get him to come to the door and went back home. After getting the full story from my daughter, I brought her down here."

Detective Sullivan turned to Patricia Ann. "Now let's hear your version, Miss. How'd you happen to be in the back yard with Mason when you were supposed to be at a girl friend's house?"

In a barely audible voice the girl said, "He . . . Mr. Mason was in the front yard when I passed on the way home. He stopped me and asked me to go back by the garage for a minute. He said . . . he said he wanted to show me something."

"And you didn't suspect what he really wanted?"

She shook her head.

"Then what happened?"

"When we got back to the garage, he just grabbed me and threw me down. I tried to fight him off, but he was too strong."

"Why didn't you scream?"

Her eyes grew wide as she stared at the detective. "I . . . I don't know," she whispered. "I guess I was too scared."

All this time Mason had been listening with increasingly mounting rage. Now he was unable to maintain silence any longer.

"Can't either of you see she's lying?" he asked.

Ignoring him, Sullivan said to Simms, "There's only one more thing we need, Mr. Simms. Who's your family doctor?"

Simms looked at him blankly. Finally he said, "Dr. Barnes, over on Eagle Street. Why?"

"Your daughter will have to be examined, of course. I suggest you run her over right now. We'll get in touch with the doctor for his report in the morning."

"But she says she isn't hurt physically," the girl's father protested. "Does she have to be subjected to further embarrassment?"

"It's the law in cases of criminal attack, Mr. Simms. She'll have to be examined either by your family doctor or a police surgeon."

"All right," Simms agreed, reluctantly. Then he had another

thought. "Does all this have to get in the papers, officer?"

"I'm afraid there isn't any way to keep it out, Mr. Simms. But you needn't worry about that. The names of minors aren't printed in criminal cases. Your daughter will be referred to in the papers merely as 'a girl high-school student.' "

"Yes," Mason said bitterly. "I'm the only one who will get the benefit of all the publicity."

When the father and daughter had left, Simms with a parting glare of hate at Mason and Pat with her eyes averted, Sullivan said to Mason, "Want to get it over with and make a statement now?"

"I want to phone my lawyer," Mason said.

The detective shrugged. "Suit yourself. But no lawyer is going to get you out of this one, Buster."

Detective Harry Sullivan's prophecy was correct to a certain extent, Mason realized during the next few days. His lawyer managed to get him out of jail on bond by morning, but he was far from out of trouble. As a matter of fact his real troubles did not start until twenty-four hours after the newspapers reported his arrest.

The arrest had been made on Monday night. Tuesday morning the first news reports appeared. As Sullivan had predicted, Patricia Ann's name did not appear at all, the papers referring to her merely as a "girl high-school senior." But Mason got plenty of publicity, including a front-page photograph beneath which appeared: COACH GERALD MASON OF WHITE RAMS CHARGED WITH CRIMINAL ATTACK.

On Wednesday morning, before Mason even got the letter containing the same news, the papers announced his contract with the White Rams had been canceled under the "good moral character" clause it contained. That afternoon Mrs. Milligan, who came in daily to clean house and cook for Mason, announced she would no longer be available.

Meantime minor repercussions as a result of his publicity were taking place. Two friends passed him on the street without speaking. The neighborhood druggist, whom he had patronized for years, bluntly refused to cash a check. But the final straw occurred on Thursday.

Thursday morning the counter man at the local restaurant Mason chose for breakfast slapped his bacon and eggs in front of him with the same air of contempt he might have exhibited in tossing a bone to a dog. Dropping a dollar on the counter, Mason quietly left without touching the food.

Getting himself an enormous supply of canned foods at a supermarket, he locked his doors, drew all the drapes in his house and retired from public view.

Late Friday afternoon Detective Harry Sullivan rang his bell.

When he opened the door, Mason

said belligerently, "What do you want? I'm not scheduled for Grand Jury action until Tuesday."

"Maybe I want to help you," Sullivan said in a mild tone. "I'd like you to come next door with me."

Mason regarded him suspiciously. "Why?"

"I think you've got a wrong slant on us cops," the detective said. "Like any humans, we've got opinions and prejudices. But we don't let them obstruct our work. In the face of Simms's testimony that he saw his daughter being attacked, and the girl's positive identification of you as the attacker, I'll admit I was convinced you were guilty. But it didn't stop me from making an impartial investigation. And now I'm not so sure. Let's go next door."

Wondering, Mason followed the detective over to his neighbor's house. They found Wendell Simms seated on his front porch.

When he saw Mason, Simms leaped to his feet and demanded, "What do you want here?"

"He's with me," Sullivan said mildly. "Where's Patricia Ann, Mr. Simms? I want to talk to her."

"Hasn't she been subjected to enough embarrassment?"

The detective's voice turned brittle. "I'm getting a little tired of you, Mr. Simms. Either go get your daughter, or I'll leave and come back with a warrant and drag her down to headquarters to talk."

Simms looked at him with his mouth open. He began to sputter, but something in the detective's expression changed his mind. Wordlessly he turned and entered the house. A few minutes later he came back with the girl.

Patricia Ann's eyes moved from Mason to the detective. Her fright seemed to accentuate her sexual defenselessness, making her seem to Mason even more physically desirable than usual, despite his anger and exasperation at her. As always when he saw the girl, he had to put a hard brake on his thoughts.

Without preamble Sullivan said, "We did some checking, young lady, and you weren't studying with Judy Merritt Monday night. Where were you?"

Her eyes grew wide and terrified. "I was too," she whispered.

Slowly the detective shook his head. "No, Patricia Ann. You lied. Where were you?"

"What is this?" Simms asked peremptorily. "Pat, what's he mean?"

Without taking his eyes from the girl's face, Sullivan said, "You shut up, Mr. Simms, and stay shut up. Your daughter lied about where she was. And if she lied about that, maybe she lied about the whole thing. I'm going to find out right now."

He continued staring at the girl while her expression grew more and more terrified. Her father, his face white, stared at her also.

Finally she whispered, "I told the truth. Except about that. I was . . .

I went to a picture show. Alone."

"What one?"

"The Regent." Suddenly her voice came with a rush. "I lied to Daddy about Judy because I knew he wouldn't let me go to a show on a school night. But the rest was true. Honest it was."

Slowly the color returned to Simms' face. He frowned at his daughter, but the frown had more relief in it than displeasure. In a curt tone he said to Sullivan, "While I don't approve of sneaky actions, sneaking off to a show, when she wasn't supposed to, isn't exactly a crime. What are you trying to prove?"

The detective swung his deliberate gaze at the father. "You know what Dr. Barnes's report said, Mr. Simms? I mean aside from saying your daughter hadn't suffered any physical harm? It said she wasn't a virgin. Not as a result of Monday night. From before that. Probably long before that."

The father's face grew pinched and white. "You're lying," he said in a voice nearly as low as the whisper of his daughter.

"No, sir. It's your daughter who's lying. I have a theory that may interest you. I think your daughter was with a boy friend Monday night. Somebody probably her own age. And I don't think she was raped. I think she was cooperating when you caught them. I think she was so scared at being caught, she jumped at the chance of passing it off as rape when she saw you took it for that."

Simms' face swung toward his daughter, and she cowered under his terrible look. When she began to whimper, his expression of accusation gradually turned to one of certainty. His features had set in a mold of restraint when he turned back to the detective.

"I'd like to take Pat inside and talk to her," he said. "I'm sure I can get the truth of this. If you'll just wait here, I won't be very long."

"All right," the detective agreed.

Simms and the girl had been gone not more than fifteen minutes when the father returned alone. His face had aged ten years in the interim.

"I want to withdraw my complaint against Mr. Mason," he said in a dull voice. "The boy is Alfred Starr, officer." His face assumed an expression of unbelieving wonder. "He's not even a senior. He's only seventeen years old."

As Mason and the detective walked away from the house, Sullivan said, "It's not part of my job to give legal advice, but you've got a beautiful defamation of character case here, Mr. Mason."

Mason laughed without humor. "I'm not interested in revenge. I just want things straightened out in the public mind."

"That's a lot to hope for."

Mason looked at him puzzledly. "What do you mean by that?"

They had reached the curb and

stopped together next to the detective's car. Sullivan said, "In twelve years on the force I've seen a lot of people convicted in the newspapers and later acquitted by the law. But the acquittal is never complete. Not that the papers won't be fair about it. They aren't out to pillory innocent people. They'll publish that the girl admitted the story was a hoax and charges against you have been dropped. But a lot of people will try to read some kind of intrigue between the lines. They'll say it was hushed up through influence because you're a well-known figure, or that you bought the kid off, and no matter what the papers report, they'll continue to think you're guilty as hell. Not everybody. But enough people so this thing will follow you the rest of your life. Oh, I imagine the White Rams will reinstate you and your friends will start talking to you again. But you never come entirely clean after a thing like this. Ten years from now when your name is mentioned, someone in the crowd is bound to say, 'Gerald Mason. Isn't he the guy who skinned out of that rape charge?' If I was in your shoes, I'd want a little monetary compensation from the guy who threw the dirt."

Mason shook his head. "I'm not interested in revenge," he repeated.

But after the detective drove away, he looked thoughtfully back at the Simms house for a long time.

That night as he sat alone on his front porch, he was still glancing at his neighbor's house with a thoughtful expression on his face. He had no doubt that the detective's bleak estimate of the future was true, and that in many minds he would forever be regarded as the man who got away with rape. Nevertheless he could not bring himself to feel anger toward Wendell Simms, for the man had acted in the sincere belief that his daughter had been attacked. It was Patricia Ann, not her father, who was the target for his resentment.

When his thoughts touched the girl, as usual an image of her ripe body formed in his mind, and the guilt the picture brought with it had the effect of partly allaying his anger. Then all at once he for the first time relaxed his mental inhibitions enough to admit to himself the girl's charge had contained a slight element of truth, even though she did not know it. For in his mind he had raped Patricia Ann repeatedly.

At ten o'clock he saw the Simms's car drive from its garage, and as it turned left to pass his house, a street lamp shining through the windshield showed him Wendell Simms and his wife attired in evening clothes.

Out for the evening, he thought with mild contempt, realizing Simms' strict sense of conformity was so complete, even the shock of learning of his daughter's immorality had not caused him to cancel whatever social event he and his wife were scheduled to attend that evening. A matter of keeping up appearances, Mason supposed.

Then it occurred to him Patricia Ann must be at home alone.

The idea formed slowly, but when it had grown to completion in his mind, he experienced no feeling of guilt whatever. His sole emotion was a sense of impending justice. Rising, he crossed the lawn between the two houses, and when he found the front door unlocked, quietly let himself into Simms' house.

He found Patricia Ann in the front room poring over school books. She thrust them aside and stood up when he entered, her face slowly turning red with a mixture of surprise and embarrassment.

Without speaking Mason deliberately drew the window drapes, then turned to look at the girl. She was dressed in a black skirt, bobby sox and flat-heeled sandals, and a thin white sweater which clung to her firm young torso as tightly as though it were a second layer of skin. Her lips parted slightly and her suddenly terrified eyes looked at him with the enormous guilt of a child who has been caught in mischief by an adult.

Mason said pleasantly, "Ever hear the story of the boy who cried, 'Wolf!' Patricia Ann?"

The girl licked her lips.

"What do you mean, Mr. Mason?

"I mean if after your father comes home, you try to tell him you were raped *again* by your next door neighbor, he'll probably take a razor strop to your behind. Don't you think that would be a natural reaction?"

"I . . . I don't know what you mean, Mr. Mason."

"It's very simple," Mason said. "There's an old adage that goes, 'If you've got the name, you may as well have the game.' "

And he advanced on her slowly.

Dead Heat

IT WAS supposed to be illegal. Lots of things are. But not for men like Lew Winters. It was easy and everything went off fine, just the way Lew planned it, just the way everything always did for him. There were no witnesses, nobody to bother us. Elco Park, the little Delaware half mile horse rink, was supposed to be closed. The summer meet had finished up two weeks ago. But for a hundred bucks Lew got the gate key from the Park super and not too many questions asked that couldn't be answered by the right lies.

We were out behind the starting gate, with dawn mists wreathing all around us. The air was chill and tangy with the smell of salt from the marshes not too far away.

I kept telling myself that this wasn't going to be too bad. I could take it. It would all be over in another couple of minutes. What the hell, it was only an animal and what was I getting in an uproar

BY

ROBERT TURNER

Winters was crooked. Matty was a good jockey. But Winters held the reins . . .

about? It didn't work. My guts stayed balled-up and hurting as though a fist clenched them. I kept spitting but it didn't get the sick sourness out of my mouth. It took me a long time to saddle-up the colt. Lew got impatient.

"Come on," he said. "Snap it up, Matty. What are you waiting for? What are you trembling about? It's not that cold. Something wrong? Something bothering you?"

I looked up at him as he lit a cigarette. His long legs were apart and he held the shotgun in the crook of his right arm, a big, handsome guy in turtle-neck sweater and jodhpurs, with his thick curly hair carefully tousled. I watched the quick flare of the cigarette lighter soften his features so that he looked almost young and boyish that moment. The lighter clicked out. He dragged on the cigarette and blew out smoke and smiled at me. It was a soft, friendly smile. The same one that framed his full mouth when he whipped a sluggish horse with a length of iron chain before bringing him out of the barn for a race.

After the tack was on the colt I kept fussing with it until Lew said: "Stop the stalling. Get him into the gate."

"Easy, Baby," I said. "Easy, Smallfry." The colt stopped shying his head and walked into one of the starting gate stalls. He stood there quietly. Lew moved behind the stall and took the single-barrel shotgun from the crook of his arm. He jacked a cartridge into the chamber and cocked the hammer.

"Ready?" he said. "Get up there."

I looked at the gun. The sickness filled me. I wanted to tell him no. I wanted to tell him what he could do with this whole idea and get away from here fast before it happened.

Still smiling, he said: "What's the matter? I told you to get up there."

I turned and walked to the end of the gate and climbed up to the assistant starter's place. I put my hand over the button that electrically controlled the gate, that sprung the stalls open in front and changed the big bell. I didn't look at Lew Winters, standing behind Smallfry with the shotgun in firing position, now. I didn't look at the colt. I just stared off into the gray mists, rigidly, trying to make my mind a blank.

"Okay," Lew said. "They're off."

I pushed the button. Simultaneously with the clang of the starting bell and the clatter of the sprung gates, the shotgun blasted. There was a piercing, almost human scream of pain as the charge of rock salt in the shotgun cartridge blasted full into the colt's hind quarters. Smallfry came out of the gate as though jet propelled. He kept going. He tore around the track, that awful tortured whinnying carried back by the wind.

Lew Winters laughed softly. He said: "Look at him go, Matty. We should have clocked him for this." He looked smug. "We won't have to worry about that skin loafing in the gate any more. Now we've got ourselves a horse. Let him go around twice and then collar him and walk him cool and bring him around to the van. I'll see you there."

I climbed down from the gate. I didn't say anything, but my eyes did; my face did. Lew saw that. He said: "You don't like me, do you? That's too damned bad. What are you going to do about it? Go ahead, take a swing. That's what you feel like doing, isn't it?"

Once I had tried that. It had been stupid. Even if I hadn't been only five feet two, a hundred and fourteen pounds. In addition to the cracked ribs and lost teeth it cost me, it also could have meant facing a murder rap on that Drisco business in Florida. He let me know that the next time I tried to get tough it would be that way. So I'd learned to control my temper. With Lew, anyhow.

Still laughing, he turned and vaulted the infield fence and headed toward the barn area. Smallfry came around the half mile track the second time, tiring. I unhitched the lead pony we'd borrowed and mounted it and went after the colt. I eased alongside of him on the clubhouse turn. I didn't look at the torn flesh of his riddled haunches but I could smell the blood and the animal was still whinnying pitifully. When I eased him to a stop he was lathered and trembling weakly. His eyes rolled in agonized terror. I got off the lead pony and walked them both and then I led them toward the barns.

In the horse van parked in the stable area, old Josh, the groom, gave the colt a hypo and then he went to work on him with the stuff in his little black bag. Josh wasn't a licensed vet but he was better than most. To him a horse's health was more important than a human's. I wondered what Lew had on him to make Josh put up with things like this.

Lew said: "What about it, Josh? How is he?" He wasn't smiling now. As he put the shotgun up on a shelf of the van, a worried frown cut between his silky brows. He pulled nervously at his lower lip, waiting for Josh to answer. He watched Josh's huge, clever brown hands put jars and tubes and bottles back into the bag. Josh straightened and sighed. His lined dark face showed nothing, no emotion. His bloodshot eyes didn't look at Lew. He said slowly:

"He be all right, I reckon. He won't be able to work out for at least a week, though. It'll be a month before he'll be fit to run right."

"That's all right," Lew's handsome face relaxed. He washed his big manicured hands together. "I can wait. What's a month? You know what this colt went off at, his last race?"

Josh ducked his head. "Seventy to one."

"Yeah." Lew looked down at the horse. He licked his lips. "You nurse him good, real good, Josh boy, and I'll give you a bundle to put on him in New York when he's ready to run."

Josh bent and lightly stroked the colt. He didn't say anything. I said: "You're sure he'll win now, aren't you, Lew? Always so damned sure about everything."

"Are you kidding?" He looked at me with disgust. "He'd have broke his maiden long ago if he'd had sense enough to get out of that gate at the bell. He's got the speed. Even trailing the pack a couple furlongs he always came at the leaders hard at the end. From now on when those gates clang open he'll remember that dose of rock salt and you couldn't hold him in there. He'll break on top and nothing will head him from wire to wire. Sure of it? Hell, I was never more sure of anything."

He was right. Smallfry was a fast colt. No handicap horse, but he could beat his own kind regularly if he broke fast. And he would now. They wouldn't bet him much either, even when his fast works got out. They'd look over his record, eight races without being better than fourth and the handicapper's comment each time, "off slowly." They'd see where the colt had been dropped down from Allowance races all the way to a thousand dollar claimer at Fair Grounds where Lew picked him up.

His previous owner had tried everything. They'd run him at a distance, hoping he could overcome that slow start. But Smallfry was strictly a sprinter. He quit after six or seven furlongs. They'd tried everything to break him of gate-laziness. Everything except a shotgun load of rock salt. There weren't many owners or trainers who would stoop that low even if getting caught wouldn't get you barred for life and a jail stretch.

"Matty," Lew said. "Get the van rolling. You know where that farm is on Long Island. Josh, keep that nosy farmer away from the colt. Just say he's sick and he can't have any strangers around him until he gets better. A couple of weeks out there and he'll be ready to barn-in with the others at Belmont and use the training track. I don't have to tell you to keep your mouth shut." He swung his blue, long-lashed eyes, cold and depthless, toward me. "Either of you."

Neither Josh nor I answered. Lew said: "I'll pick Lila up at the hotel and drive on ahead. Matty, I'll see you at the barn in the morning. We're going to work out The Piper."

He turned and jumped down out of the van. I watched him get into his lavender Lincoln convertible and drive off. Lila. I got sick to my stomach every time her name came out of his mouth. Sweat broke out as I thought about him going back to that Inn in the village and Lila probably still in bed, that sensual little bud of a mouth so prettily swollen with sleep. I thought about Lew Winters waking her and the way he'd do that and how it'd probably be at least a couple of hours after that before they got on the road. Sweat poured from me and I ached with a crazy mixture of hate and desire.

I wiped my hands on the sides of my levis and went around and climbed up into the cab of the horse van.

Somewhere in Pennsylvania we stopped for a beer and hamburger and Josh got up to ride in the cab with me for awhile. We didn't talk at first. We seldom did. But I guess what Lew had done to that poor colt rubbed raw with Josh, too. He said:

"Matty, I'm going to tell you a secret. I've had it. This mornin' was the end. After I get this colt nursed back to health in New York, I'm all through. No more Mr. Winters for ol' Josh. I'm gettin' out from under."

I hid my surprise. I said: "What'll you do then?"

"I dunno for sure." He sighed. "I got a daughter in Harlem and friends. Good friends. Mr. Winters been holdin' a probation-jump on me but I don't even care no more. Better to go back on a Carolina road gang than to keep on gettin' sick in the guts workin' for a man like him." His voice got low and rough-sounding and taut. "But before I take off I'm goin' to fix Mr. Lew Winters. Fix him good and for all. You wait and see. Real good so he won't shotgun no more poor he'pless beasts."

I didn't answer. I didn't know whether he was just talking or not. I'd never heard Josh blow off before, though. He was quiet for awhile and then he said: "None of my business, Matty, but how come you stay with him? Year ago, before you started to ride for Mr. Winters, exclusively, you was doin' way better. You was leading apprentice and free-lancing, with your pick of mounts. You was doin' fine, just fine. You sure ain't done so hot with Mr. Winters. And one of these days them patrol judges goin' to clobber you for pullin' a horse when Mr. Winters bettin' against his own entry. It just don't figger."

I kept my eyes on the road and didn't answer. He took the hint and began to talk about something else. But it was a little too late. He'd got me thinking, remembering again the morning Lew Winters approached me a year ago.

I saw him coming toward me after the workouts and I looked the other way. It wasn't smart for an honest rider to be seen even talking to a trainer with his rep. He said:

"Matty, I'd like you to work for me. I could use a hot-riding kid like you."

I shook my head. "Sorry. I'm tied up for the rest of this meet."

"Are you, Matty? I don't think so. I think you're going to change your mind. You'll like riding for me, too. You won't even want to bother with anybody else. You seem like a kid who can take orders and not ask too many questions, either. We'll get along fine."

"I just told you, I can't —"

"Matty," he cut me off. He was looking across the track toward the small lake in the infield. "You seemed awful nervous all day yesterday. Didn't ride as well as usually. And this morning you look as though maybe you didn't sleep much last night. Something bothering you?"

"No," I said. There was suddenly a feeling like crawling things along my backbone. I didn't like the cocky, assured way he was going at this. Nor the way he was staring at that lake.

"Say," he said, turning suddenly toward me. His eyes seemed to go right through me. "I hear that crazy stable boy, Al Drisco, left sometime yesterday. Just quit his job and took off without saying anything to anybody. At least they think that's what he did."

I felt my legs go weak. I tried to get my eyes away from his but they wouldn't seem to go. I didn't say anything. Still smiling, Winters went on: "He was a handsome boy, that Drisco. Hear he fancied himself quite a romeo. Women were nuts about him. And if he couldn't get 'em any other way, he didn't mind doing a little strong-arming. Heard he served time up north for attacking a trainer's wife, in a barn early one morning. You know what's going to happen to a guy like that some day, Matty? Some guy's going to catch him messing around with his wife or his girl and crack his head open for him. Don't you think so, Matty?"

I knew then. I was pretty sure. We'd been wrong, Lila and I. Somebody *had* seen us yesterday morning, lugging Al Drisco's corpse over the infield lake to get rid of it. We hadn't got away with it.

"What's the matter, Matty?" Winters asked. "You look a little pale. That Drisco guy been bothering that cute little dame you go around with? That Lila kid?"

I couldn't answer him. I tried to, but my mouth was all dry and shriveled inside and my tongue felt swollen. I kept seeing what had happened the morning before. Lila had come out to the track with me early for the morning workouts. She'd waited in the stable area while I'd changed clothes in the jockey's quarters. It was a foggy morning and few people were around. When I came back, this Al Drisco, this big handsome stable-boy goon, had Lila backed up in the corner of an empty stall, one hand over her mouth so she couldn't holler. I got one look at what he was doing with his other hand and the flushed, bestial, drunken look on his face and I went berserk. Even when he started to fall I didn't stop hitting him with the weighted end of my riding stick.

Lila had said we could get away with it, since I'd only been protecting her from his attack. But I didn't like the looks of it. He'd managed not to tear her clothes. There would only be our word on that. Once when I was a kid I spent six months in a reform school. I swore then I'd never go to jail for anything. Not anything.

We talked it over, hurriedly and I remembered that Drisco was known around the tracks as a drifter. Nobody would much care or do any investigating if he just disappeared. I thought about the lake. I talked Lila into it. Now I realized how stupid it had been. Now, when it was too late.

"See you're sporting a new bat, kid," Lew Winters said. He looked down at the new riding whip I'd bought the day before. "What happened to the old one, that special made one with your initials on it?"

I didn't answer. I didn't have to. He knew what had happened to it, if he knew the rest. He'd seen me throw the blood stained thing into the lake after we'd weighted down Drisco's corpse and tossed it into the water.

"Matty," he said. "You'd better cancel all other mounts after this afternoon. Tell your agent you're signing with me. We don't need any contract, do we? We can trust each other."

He turned then and started away. After a few steps he called back: "Oh, yes, Matty. Tell your little friend, Lila, she'll be traveling with us. Tell her to come around to my hotel and talk to me, tonight. I have a job for her. I need a — secretary."

I wanted to run after him right then and kill him. It seemed he was one jump ahead of me all the time. "And, Matty," he said. "Don't get any ideas about more violence. Last night I wrote a little story, a little murder story about a corpse hidden in a lake. It's in a sealed envelope with my attorney, to be opened only upon my death. You understand, Matty?"

He went around the corner of the barns, then, and out of sight. I saw Lila that morning and told her about this. She was scared. He really had us. The real story of what had happened with Drisco would never stand up, now, after we'd hidden the body. That night Lila went over to Winter's hotel. She said she was going to try and talk him out of putting the pressure on us like that, tell him what had really happened and why. She thought he might feel sorry for us, then. She should've known better, a guy who would do something like that in the first place.

I never saw Lila alone again after that. The night she called me up and told me that we were through, she and I, and that she never wanted to see me again. I could hear the choking in her voice and Lew Winters' chuckling in the background. I went over to his hotel after she hung up on me. Winters made her tell the house dick that I was annoying them. They had me thrown out.

For a year, now, I'd hardly seen Lila. The few times I did, she kept her eyes away from mine. She couldn't look at me. A year of Lew Winters having the girl I'd been going to marry. A year of that and of riding the way he told me to ride, of pulling every crooked trick in the book. I didn't know how much longer I could take it. The business with Smallfry this morning showed me how tight the strain of the whole thing was getting. It would break soon. I had that feeling. I didn't know when or how or what would happen, but I knew something was going to break.

The third week in New York, they brought the colt from the farm, where Lew had sent him to recuperate, to the barns at Belmont. Smallfry was healed now and seemed none the worse for the rock salt treatment unless you knew him well. He was nervous, as though he'd been trained a shade too fine. And there was always a sort of wild, panicky gleam in his eye.

After he brought Smallfry back from the farm, old Josh, the groom, took off, just as he'd said he would. He didn't show up for work the next morning. Lew was in an ugly mood about that. I tried to placate him. I said: "What difference does it make, now that Smallfry's all healed? You don't need Josh. You can get another groom."

"Don't be stupid," Lew told me. "I can get along without him right now. But if this Smallfry trick works the way I think it's going to, I'll pull it again. There are other horses around that can take a race if they get suddenly cured of gate-slowness. Now I'll have to find another guy who knows how to dig rock salt out of a horse's hide and keep his mouth shut at the same time. It won't be easy."

I thought about what Josh had said about fixing Lew before he left, fixing him so he'd never be able to do that to a horse again. I figured Josh must've forgot about that, or else just decided that running out on Lew was satisfaction enough.

The first morning I worked the colt out, he was stiff. He was hard to handle too but I finally got him gentled down. Later that week he breezed through the morning works in better than average time. The following week he worked six furlongs in a blazing 1:14. Some races aren't run any faster.

That day Lew said: "He's ready, kid. He's sharp now. Saturday I drop him into a five thousand dollar claimer at seven furlongs. Every entry has won at least one other heat. Except Smallfry. He'll be a big price, a real big price."

I didn't say anything. I tried to figure some way Lew could be wrong. If only he could be wrong about something for once. Especially something big like this. But he wouldn't be. Several times we'd gone to the track early and broken Small-fry from the gate when nobody was around. The association worked. He came away from the barrier like a roman candle the second the bell rang and the gates flashed open. And he had the speed to beat the rest of the pigs that would be in that race. There was no question about this being the sure thing Lew had it tabbed for.

That afternoon I didn't have any mounts in the late races and went back to Manhattan early. Lew stayed out at the track to watch some of the competition we were going to meet Saturday run in the Eighth.

At my hotel desk there was a message for me to call Lila. I went crazy with excitement. It was the first time that she'd made any effort to get in touch with me. I decided to hell with the phone. I went out and took a cab over to the swank Park Avenue hotel where Lew lived.

I knocked on the door of their suite. There was a soft shuffle of footsteps inside, coming toward the door. Then the door opened and there she was. My neck suddenly felt swollen and I could feel blood beating through all the veins in my head. She must have thought it was Lew come home early because she was wearing only the tops of red satin Chinese lounging pajamas. They covered her high about the throat and shimmered across the quivering stain of her breasts. Long chestnut colored hair was brushed loose and shiny about her shoulders. I'd forgotten how tall she was and how widely set were her almond-shaped black eyes, how incredibly thick and long her lashes were. Her mouth was sullen and moist.

Pushing past her into the room, I slammed the door. I leaned against it and let my eyes go over her. I could hear the loud sound of my own breathing. She backed away from me. She looked down at me and said: "Matty, you — you shouldn't have come here. You should have just called. We —"

"It's too late for that. I'm here. What is it, Lila? Why did you want to talk to me?"

The flat of her hands kept moving down the sides of her thighs. She kept tugging at the hem of the pajama top, trying to make it longer. It didn't do much good. Her legs were white and long and beautiful.

"Matty," she said. "I — I learned something today. Something important. I had to tell you."

I hardly heard what she said. Being close to her again after so long, being here alone with her again after all that time, was the only thing in my mind. "What?" I said. "What is it?"

She told me twice before the words sunk in and I realized their import. Lew's lawyer had called today while Lew was out. Lila had talked with him. During the conversation, in desperation, she'd asked him about the envelope Lew had left to be opened in the advent of his death. She'd tried to trick the lawyer into sending it over to the hotel, told him that Lew wanted it back. And that was when she found out that there was no such envelope.

"He was lying about that, Matty," she said, excitedly. "Bluffing, to make sure you didn't kill him to shut him up about the Drisco business."

I looked at her and thought about that and that it meant that now, if I wanted to, I *could* kill him and shut him up forever. And get Lila back. All this would be over. I said, softly:

"Lila, tell me something straight. How — how has it been? I mean, Lew's a big, good looking guy. You've had the best of everything. Maybe you don't want out, now?"

"Matty!" Her eyes got hurt. "You're crazy. You don't know what you're saying. I still love you, Matty. With him I've been only a — a wooden woman. Nothing, none of this being with him the past year has meant anything."

"That's all I want to know, Lila," I said. "Come here."

She backed away from me. "No, Matty. He might come back here early and catch you here. He —"

"So what?" I said. "I don't care, now." I walked toward her, my eyes going all over her, and this time she didn't back away.

It was much later when I left their hotel room but Lew still hadn't gotten back. And I had a new idea, now. I wasn't going to be satisfied with just killing Lew Winters. First I was going to pay him back a little for this year of hell. I was going to fix his wagon, ruin him completely, before I killed him. Put the big sweat on him, for at least a little while before he died. I was going to do that in the race, Saturday, the race Smallfry was supposed to win, the big killing that Lew had looked forward to making for so long.

Everything went off just the way Lew planned it in that race, Saturday. Smallfry was fifty to one on the board and Lew had ten thousand bucks riding on his nose. When the starting bell yammered and the gates jacked open, the colt went out of there as though he was catapulted. Another fast starter, Krazykat, was right with him, maybe a head back. I made no effort to hold Smallfry in. I couldn't have if I'd wanted to. Nobody could hold him once he broke from a barrier since that dose of rock salt.

I didn't worry about this Krazykat, either, even though he stayed right with us, along the rail, several lengths ahead of the pack, head and head all the way to the stretch. I knew I could take the race any time I wanted to make a move. The boy on Krazykat was larruping away with the whip, forcing his mount to the utmost just to stay with me. I hadn't pressed Smallfry yet. One flick of the bat and he'd surge ahead as though Krazykat was standing still. I knew that, and that we'd stay that way, then, right to the wire and we'd be in and Lew Winters would have made half a million.

He was following the progress of the race through his binocs, I knew. I imagined how he was feeling. By now he knew we were going to take it for sure, just as he'd planned. There was no way we could lose. I grinned into the whipping wind. I wished I could see Lew Winters' face in the next few seconds.

Savagely I lashed Smallfry with the bat. He shivered and leaped ahead and began to pull away from the black colt on the rail. Then I fixed Lew Winters. For no reason and still close enough to force Krazykat to pull up hard, I cut over in front of him to the rail. It was a deliberate foul. The judges couldn't miss spotting it. I heard the screamed oaths of the boy on the other colt and then I flicked Smallfry with the bat again and we sailed down under the wire, winning by plenty of daylight.

Riding back to the Winner's Circle and the weigh-out, I glanced up at the tote board and saw the red neon flash the word *Objection.* I listened to the announcer tell the crowd to hold onto their tickets, that a foul had been claimed. Just outside the winner's circle, I dismounted and Lew Winters and the new groom came out to help me strip the tack from the colt and to blanket him and lead him to the barn.

Lew Winters's dead-white face looked like something made of putty that had been squeezed. He could hardly talk. All he could say was: "You slimy little bastard, you did that deliberately. I'll fix you for this. I'll fix you good."

Then I was taken up to the judges' stand along with the boy who'd claimed the foul. Films of the race were run off and the foul claim was sustained. Smallfry's number was taken down from the win slot on the tote board and Krazykat's put in its place. I got a lecture from the officials and they set me down for thirty days for careless riding. Not that it mattered.

I got dressed in the jockey's quarters and took from my locker the big springblade knife I'd bought the night before and the pair of gloves. I wiped the knife off carefully and put on the gloves. Then I went looking for Lew Winters. It took me awhile to find him. He was in the horse van, out behind the barns, getting it ready for a trip. I knew what he had in mind. He was going to ship Smallfry to some other track, quickly, and try again to cash in on him, before word of this race got around. He was all alone there in the horse van.

"Lew," I said. He was at the far end of the van. He couldn't get past me to get out. He turned around. He looked at the knife in my gloved right hand, jerked a little at the sound of the blade springing free.

I was suddenly soaked with sweat all over. I felt a little sick to my stomach. I wondered now if I'd be able to go through with this. Killing Al Drisco in a fit of anger had been different. This was going to be cold and deliberate. I kept trying not to think about the blade sliding into him and the way his face would look when he died. I kept thinking about Lila and telling myself that this had to be, that it was the only way. "How was it, Lew?" I said. "How did it feel when you saw me commit that foul, lose the race that way for you? And all that money? Spread all over so you wouldn't hurt the odds. You never thought I'd pull anything like that, did you?"

"You — you're out of your mind," he said. He snapped the words out and spittle sprayed from his mouth. "You must be. You know what will happen if you try to kill me." I shook my head.

"No, it won't, Lew. Lila and I found out. There is no envelope. You figured just the bluff would be enough to keep you safe. So now I can do this, Lew. Lila and I are getting out from under."

His eyes darted around the van as I moved slowly toward him. Then they stopped, staring at a rack on the wall, a few feet to his left. I looked too. I saw the shotgun there just as he lunged toward it, snatched it down from the wall. I ran at him, trying to get to him with the knife before he could squeeze the trigger. But I was still several feet away from him when the gun went off with an ear-splitting blast of sound.

For a moment I was blinded by the flash of its explosion. Then the smoke cleared away and I saw that Lew Winters was no longer holding the shotgun in his hand. It was no longer a gun. It was just a splintered stock and pieces of broken metal scattered all around him and with a good part of it embedded into his face, along with wads of shot that had blasted back at him when the gun blew up in his hands. His whole head and face was a gory mess. There was a big hole burned through the shirt and into his chest. I watched his legs go out from under him.

"Josh," I said, remembering what the old groom had said about fixing Lew so he'd never shotgun another horse. "He did fix Lew. But good. He stuffed up the barrel of the gun, knowing damned well that someday Lew would use it to break another horse of gate-slowness."

I turned away, then, peeling off the gloves and putting the switch-blade knife back in my pocket. I went out of the van. I thought about Lila, waiting back there in the hotel, all packed and ready to leave with me for Mexico. Right up to the end, she'd pleaded with me not to kill Lew. She'd said there must be some other way, even though she would go along with me my way. I thought how glad she'd be to learn that she was right. There had been another way.

It was lots of fun, everybody agreed. And then, suddenly, somebody screamed.

BY

HAROLD CANTOR

The Idiot

I WAS having another dream about Marion — a beaut, this time. She was walking down a long ramp toward a Greyhound bus, walking out of my life, swinging her model's hat-box. I knew I had to stop her, but my feet were stuck and I couldn't move.

A gust of wind raised her skirt, exposing her shapely nyloned legs and the white of her thighs. The bus driver looked her up and down, reached to help her, and Marion smiled up at him, invitingly . . .

I woke up, sweating and frustrated. I slipped out of bed into my tennis sneakers, put on my shorts and went outside. Ernie was standing on the porch of his bungalow — the one opposite mine — holding a candid camera.

"Morning, Mr. Carson," he called cheerfully, blinking at me through his thick-rimmed glasses.

"Morning, Ernie," I said, and looked up at the Adirondacks sun beating down on our row of bungalows, pride of *Happy Dell — Resort for Adults.*

"I'm taking a picture of the linden tree," he said, and thumped his chest proudly. "From twenty angles!"

I nodded. Ernie was always doing things like that. It gave him something to talk about.

"I'll let you see the pictures when I've developed them, Mr. Carson," he said. "You can tell me what you think."

There was a two-day growth of beard on Ernie's face, which made you do a double-take when you heard him talk. It was like seeing a movie with Clark Gable where they dub in the voice of Roddy McDowell.

Ernie stared at me with that peculiar vacant expression of his — always most vacant when he was thinking furiously. "Are you playing tennis this morning, Mr. Carson?" he asked.

I nodded.

"With Marion?"

I nodded again — this time suspiciously.

"Can I go along, Mr. Carson? I won't bother you."

I started to shake my head. I didn't want him along when I was with Marion. She teased him without realizing what she was doing, and for some reason it annoyed the hell out of me.

Ernie pleaded. "Please, Mr. Carson. I'll take both your pictures when you play. I'll use my high speed shutter. Please, Mr. Carson?"

I kicked an orange peel from the porch and forced a smile. I didn't know how to refuse him.

"All right," I told him. "Be down at the courts in half an hour."

His face lit up with happiness. "You're my friend, Mr. Carson."

I went inside the bungalow without a word. That kind of gratitude makes me sick.

When I had poured myself a cup of coffee and buttered a few rolls, I sat down to eat my breakfast. Between gulps and bites I thought about Ernie.

As a police reporter I've come in contact with enough nuts and crackpots to make your skin crawl. I've seen the ones who spend their evenings spitting into their hands and the ones that try to catch moonbeams with their bedsheets. And I never batted an eyelash. I think what bothered me about Ernie was his being so close to normal. People should be either poor or rich, stupid or clever, sane or insane. It's easier to figure them that way. But Ernie, 20 physically, was ten years behind himself mentally. That made him neither here nor there as far as I was concerned.

I couldn't understand his parents taking him out to a resort like *Happy Dell.* Maybe they hoped he might miraculously mature if they dropped him into *Happy Dell's* social whirl. Maybe they needed a vacation. I don't know. But I do know it was a bad move. People couldn't really take to Ernie because he slowed them up. He was like a tugboat beside a cruiser. . . .

After breakfast I got my tennis racket out of the closet and went to meet Marion. For the most part *Happy Dell* was still asleep as I hurried down the dirt road which led towards the courts. Marion was over near the entrance when I arrived — with Ernie. She'd thrown her jacket across a bench and was posing for him in her white tennis outfit. Both her hands rested on the back of the bench; her body was arched and her breasts were taut . . .

The first time I'd seen Marion was at the pool. I was pulling myself out of the water when I saw this pair of legs going by and, right off, I knew what I wanted. She had a walk — and even when she stood still, she moved. She combed her hair like it was you stroking it, and she had a way of staring right through you when she spoke.

By nightfall we were dancing cheek-to-cheek, and after a few drinks it was like we had always known each other. A little after midnight we headed for my bungalow. Marion went willingly, and all I can say is — there are some things you don't forget easily.

But in the morning, when I awoke, Marion was gone. There was a note saying she had made a date a couple of days before and that it would look funny and cause talk if the guy called and she wasn't at her bungalow. It made sense, sure, but still I felt like I'd been kicked in the guts. Maybe because she made too much sense. Suddenly all I wanted was Marion: I wanted her to cling . . . I wanted to hear her say again and again that it had never been like this before, never. . . .

Marion stopped posing for Ernie and smiled at me when I came over.

"Look, Ernie," she said, "it's Mr. Stick-in-the-mud!"

I tried to grin cheerfully, but it didn't come off.

"Did you say 8:30 in the morning?" Marion said sarcastically, "or did you say 8:30?"

"I was shaving," I lied.

Marion gave a little pout to show her disbelief and sidled up to Ernie. "I wish," she said, patting him tenderly on the cheek, "that all men were as honest as you are, Ernie!"

Ernie puffed up his chest at the compliment. He opened his mouth to say something and nothing came out. I began to unscrew the brace on my racket and looked away.

"Leave the kid alone," I said.

Marion put her hands on her hips and her lower lip took on a stubborn angle. "Not yet, Kit. Ernie's going to take our pictures. Ernie's my boyfriend, aren't you, Ernie?"

He began to fumble for his camera, awkwardly moving backwards on his skinny legs.

"I'm not in the mood for pictures," I told her. "Do you want to play tennis or don't you?"

"I want to take a picture. If you don't want to be in one with me, Ernie does. Just be kind enough to snap it for us."

She grasped Ernie by the hand and drew him toward the bench. If you've ever seen the wild look in an animal's eye when they lead him to the slaughter block, then you know the way Ernie looked. Marion held her head high and put her arm about him and said in that voice of hers, "Thatta boy, Ernie. We'll make a man of you yet . . ."

One look at the calf-like worship in his eyes and I blew my top. A stupid thing to do.

"Listen, Ernie," I shouted, "why don't you go home?"

I handed his camera to him abruptly. He stared at me blankly, trying to understand what I meant.

"Go home," I repeated. "Scram. Stop hanging around!"

Involuntarily he stepped backwards, his large eyes bulging in fear. Marion moved to his side.

"What's the matter with you, Kit? What's wrong?"

"Why do you want to fool him? What good does it do!"

A slow flush rose to Marion's cheeks. For a minute I thought she was going to understand, but then she shrugged her shoulders and picked up her jacket from the bench.

"Come along, honey," she said, taking Ernie by the arm. "You're still my sweetheart. Don't let Kit bully you. He just forgot to get up this morning."

I watched the two of them walk down the dirt road. I could tell from the tilt of Marion's head and the way she walked that she might be angry for days. That was the worst part of it.

I picked up a tennis ball and began tossing it up in the air. There was no logical way to account for what had happened. I almost never lose my temper, and the funny thing was that I really liked Ernie. It's just that I had my own theories about what was good for him. Marion wasn't. "Oh, brother!" I thought. "Acting jealous of a mentally retarded kid. You first-class jerk! Soon you'll be checking with a psychiatrist."

I took my racket and walked to the center of the clay court. I hit the ball as hard as I could. The dust jumped. Then it settled. . . .

That night I made up my mind to stay put and give Marion a chance to cool off. From my bungalow you can see the lights of the clubhouse farther on down the hill and hear the cars whizzing along on the state highway nearby.

Happy Dell was whooping it up that night because it was Saturday. I listened for about five minutes to the shouts and laughter before my resistance gave way. I figured I might just as well have a few drinks. Why waste a cool summer night?

The clubhouse was jammed when I entered. I said hello to a few people and sat down in a well-padded chair by the window. The place wasn't much for looks — a few sofas, a juke box and a fireplace they use in winter for roasting hot dogs. It's big and roomy enough for dancing, but the big attraction is the liquor. They sell the stuff so cheap you ignore the taste.

I lit a cigarette and looked the crowd over. The juke box had begun playing a slow foxtrot when I saw Marion. She was dancing with a tall guy who was holding her in that clothes-presser grip that passes for dancing. Marion's eyes met mine over his shoulder and, instead of of giving me the freeze, she smiled and winked at me.

I got up from my chair like I'd been stuck by a loose spring. I cut in on Marion and grabbed her tight. It was a good feeling. I said, "Forget about this morning, honey. I must have swallowed one of my razor blades."

"Kit, I like you," she giggled. "You're just a sensitive big dope, but I like you."

We could have said more, but we didn't. We just danced. Tonight I knew I could have her, and the less talk the less chance of an argument. It was a game with her, and all I had to do was play it her way. I fully intended to.

After a few fast rhumbas, she announced that she was tired of dancing and wanted to do something *different*. We were standing a few yards from a group of people clustered around a sofa, talking in low, conspiratorial tones. Ernie's name was mentioned once or twice, and Marion nudged me closer. As soon as I saw Danny in the group I knew something was up.

Everybody at *Happy Dell* knows Danny. He's our comedian — the lad who makes all the funny sayings and keeps things moving. I think you know the kind I mean. When you were a kid, there was probably someone on your block who hung by his feet from a two-story window on a bet or just to prove he had nerve. That was Danny's way of fooling around.

When he noticed Marion and me, he said, "Here's a hot combo — Kit Carson and Maid Marion. This way to Sherwood Forest, kids. . . ." And he made us an extravagant salaam. The men standing around smiled and some of the girls snickered. Danny was short and chunky, a small man who could fill a room with his presence.

"What's up?" I asked. "What's this about Ernie?"

"Give my friend Kit a drink," Danny said.

Somebody put a glass in my hand and I didn't refuse. Again I asked my question about Ernie.

"Should we tell him?" Danny asked with a big wink.

A blonde, perched on the edge of her chair and about ready to pass out, began to giggle. "Tell him!"

Danny moved closer to me. "Ernie's in love!" he confided.

I swallowed my drink in two short gulps. He wasn't telling me anything new.

"So what?" I asked.

"So Ernie's been asking me," Danny said, going into a little dance, "about the birds, the bees and the flowers." He picked an imaginary flower from the sofa, buzzed over it and chirped three times. Everybody laughed.

"Tell him about the widow from Waterboro, Danny!" The eager, prompting voice was Marion's — and it surprised me.

"Ah, yes, the widow!" Danny said. "She wants to meet Ernie. She's waiting in my chambers."

"What widow?" I asked, "What's the gag?"

"Haven't you met her?" Danny asked. He began to sachez across the room, waving his handkerchief and taking little, mincing steps with his feet. He did it better than most girls. The blonde started giggling again and almost dropped her glass. "Gee, Danny," she said, "you're a scream!"

Maybe I'm slow on the uptake, but it didn't come across at first. I'd seen Danny do his female impersonations before, like the one with the wig and the straw hat and the buck teeth. But I never thought he'd pull something like this. They had the whole thing rigged up among them.

At 10 o'clock, Harry, who's always playing the straight man for Danny, brought Ernie into the clubhouse. Ernie had his best Saturday night suit on, and his cheeks were freshly shaven. He was biting his lip nervously and I could see the scared look in his eyes under the heavy glasses.

"Ready, my boy?" Danny asked.

Ernie nodded slowly. He didn't look ready for anything. He didn't even notice me standing there. He looked like a frightened explorer about to embark on the most dangerous trip of his career.

The light suddenly burst in my foggy brain and I turned to Marion angrily. "Listen, are you going to let them — ?" Her finger pressed to my lips silenced me. She snuggled close, squeezing my arm tightly. "Honey, don't be a *kill-joy*," she pleaded. "It's only a little joke, and you'll spoil it for everybody if you tell him."

I clenched my teeth together, remembering the fight Marion and I had had that morning. I'd tried to help Ernie then, only it hadn't done anyone any good. And I thought about that darkened bedroom in my bungalow, waiting, and how Marion would light up the place and, for the life of me, I couldn't say a word.

Danny wasn't wasting any time, anyhow. He whispered something in Ernie's ear, while he held up five fingers behind his back. That was to indicate to his friends how much time he wanted. Then, he bounded for the door, a polished actor conscious of his audience. He lifted one finger dramatically, said "Presto-change-oh!" and disappeared amid howls of laughter.

Five minutes later Marion made me take her to Danny's bungalow, where there were about 20 people gathered in the shadows outside. It's a two-story bungalow with a garden surrounding it and a picket fence in the back. Couples kept strolling down the path all the time. All the girls were tugging at the men, trying to make them turn back, but you could see they weren't tugging too hard. The hum of voices in the garden was broken now and then by a high-pitched female laugh. Ernie's name was on everybody's lips, and yet nobody seemed to know what was going on.

Suddenly, the voices stopped humming. Somebody whispered, "He's coming!" and everyone stepped back into the shadows. Nobody actually hid, but you couldn't distinguish anyone clearly in spite of the moonlight. I was the only one that remained in the path. Marion hissed angrily at me to get out of sight, but I didn't move. I couldn't. The kid had that damned habit of calling me *his friend*.

When Ernie came up the path assisted by two of Danny's pals, I knew he was past all help. The sweat was running down the side of his face and all over his collar. They practically dragged him over the threshold as though he were an unwilling bride. We all waited impatiently in the garden for a few seconds. Everyone felt obliged to speak in whispers.

"What's he doing in there?" somebody asked.

A youngster in a Hawaiian shirt tripped over a flower bed and started to curse. Somebody climbed the picket fence and tried to peer into the window.

"What's Danny doing?"

"I don't know. I can't see anything."

"Neither can Ernie!"

The pie-eyed blonde began to giggle again. Harry, Danny's straight man, came running down the path towards the bungalow. There was a little fat man with him whom I'd never seen before. He was completely bald, and moonlight bounced off the top of his head. I found out later he was somebody's visiting cousin. Harry was talking excitedly to him.

"Have you got it all straight, Max?" he asked.

"Leave it to me," the fat man said. He crossed his fingers for luck and waved to the crowd. Then, he walked straight to the door, clenched his fist and banged on it three times as hard as he could.

"Who's in there?" he called, "Who's in there with my wife?"

For a shocked second, there was silence . . . then, the laughter began. There was just no getting away from it — it *was* funny. I fought it for a minute, and then I started to laugh myself. I laughed until I thought my sides would split in two. The blonde sat down suddenly in the road and giggled hysterically. The kid in the Hawaiian shirt threw himself full-length across the flowerbed and laughed himself into a fit.

Then, Ernie opened the door and ran out. His hair was tangled, his glasses were falling off and his eyes were wild and frightened. He believed he'd been in a room with another man's wife and that her husband was after him. He ran wildly down the road and a few people followed him, shouting, "Run, Ernie!" and "He's after you, Ernie!" as loud as they could. It was a crazy, dizzy night — and I was part of the pack, howling just like the others, until — suddenly — I became aware of Marion beside me.

What hit me was the way *she* was laughing. It was clear, silvery, mocking laughter, and there was no pity in it. When I heard her laugh, the whole thing didn't seem funny any more. I started back towards the clubhouse.

Gradually, everyone who had seen the hoax drifted back in. They threw themselves down in the comfortable chairs, mixed some more drinks and talked about it. It was really the greatest gag since vaudeville. It was one of those stories you never believe when someone else is telling it. Even now, you had only to look at the person opposite you and both of you would burst out laughing just thinking about it.

Ten minutes later, when Danny made his entrance, they gave him a tremendous ovation. Marion greeted him with a kiss. His cronies clapped him on the back, made jokes and called him lover boy. There was a crazy glint in Danny's eyes, though outwardly he pretended to be shrugging the whole thing off.

Things were quieting down again when someone cleared his throat and we all looked up and there was Ernie. He had an ugly bruise on his left forearm and his clothes were torn from running through the woods. I don't know how he decided in his slow-thinking way to come back to the clubhouse. Maybe he thought he'd be safer with us. Anyhow, nobody said anything when he came in. His large eyes rolled around in their sockets and little rivers of sweat trickled down his neck. He looked desperately from one person to another until his eyes lighted on me. I think it was the first time he saw me that evening.

"Please, Mr. Carson," he said, coming forward. "He's after me!"

"Take it easy, Ernie," I said, trying to think fast, "It's all over."

Ernie sat down beside me on the sofa. He was trembling.

"You won't let him do anything?" he begged. "You're my friend!"

Everyone was staring at me, waiting for me to answer. If I said the wrong thing, I would ruin the greatest gag in *Happy Dell's* history.

Marion pouted at me and put her fingers across her lips, demanding silence. I couldn't think of a single clever remark.

"Take it easy, Ernie," I repeated. "Everything'll be okay."

Ernie clasped his hands together and unclasped them. He looked around him nervously. "Tell him I wasn't out of the house all evening, I was developing pictures. You know that's my hobby."

I didn't think he was lying. He really believed that he hadn't left the house at all. It was getting a little too rough for my skin.

"Listen, Ernie . . ." I began to open up, but Danny interrupted me. He pointed toward the doorway.

"Look who's here!"

Harry was just entering with Max. The little fat man looked like a comic character when you saw him in the full light. He advanced toward Ernie with ferocious, threatening gestures, though a smile was playing at the corners of his mouth. I felt relieved. I thought they would scare him and get another laugh and then they would explain. But I didn't figure on Danny.

"Look out, Ernie!" he shouted hoarsely, "He's got a knife!"

Ernie bolted to his feet. I realized, sickly, that he actually thought he saw that knife in the fake husband's hand. The animal look came into his eyes again and he started to run, moaning his terror to himself. Stumbling and panting, he dashed to the door and made his escape. I don't think he knew where he was going or had any idea of the direction he took. Harry followed him to see where he went.

Some of the people in the room attempted to laugh, but it wasn't as funny as the last time. You can run a good thing down. I got sore.

"Wise guy!" I said to Danny, "Enough's enough!"

"What's the matter?" he said. "No sense of humor?"

It got up to take a slug at him. I had never liked him, particularly, and I was sick of his jokes. When I think back on it, I'm sorry that I didn't hit him, but there wasn't time for it because just then we heard Harry yelling from the road. His voice came from pretty far away, but even at that distance we could sense the terror in it.

All of us began running again — me, Marion, Danny, the fat man Max, the drunken blonde, the kid in the Hawaiian shirt — we all ran like hell after Ernie. Only this time, we wanted to catch up with him and explain the whole thing and tell him we were only kidding. But when we reached the road where Harry was, there was a car parked on the side and two headlights glaring through the darkness. Ernie lay on the ground, his frightened eyes staring up at us, but not seeing anything . . .

They picked him up and carried him over to the grass. He wasn't pretty to look at because he had a fractured skull and I think his spine was broken, but I'm not sure. Danny ran for a doctor. He had to run for something because we all began staring at him.

The driver of the car was a little guy who wore glasses something like Ernie's. He kept walking around with a pencil and a notebook explaining things.

"The idiot came running out like a shot. I didn't even see him until I was on top of him."

I stooped to examine Ernie more closely. His body was crumpled in a heap on the grass, his head twisted off to one side and his mouth wide open. Except for his glasses being off, he looked exactly as I remembered him living, vacant-eyed and very much out-of-place. He didn't even look any smarter than he had before.

I felt myself getting sick and dizzy, so I walked a little way down the road to a small bridge over a gulley stream. I stopped on it and looked down at the water.

Somebody touched my shoulder and I turned around. Marion had followed me. She was crying softly into a handkerchief, and her hair looked out of place for the first time since I'd known her.

"Kit," she whispered, "I want to . . ."

"Keep away from me! Keep the goddamn hell away from me!"

I turned and faced the stream. I don't know what Marion thought. It didn't matter much. For a time, I could hear her breathing heavily, and then I heard her footsteps as she walked away. After that, it was quiet, except for the sound of crickets chirping.

Portrait of a Killer

No. 5—Louise Peete

BY DAN SONTUP

FIVE PEOPLE — a woman and four men — died because of her, but Louise Peete actually murdered only two of them. The other three committed suicide.

The first one to go was Harry Faurote, her second husband. His was perhaps the simplest death of them all. Louise deserted him after a quick marriage, and Harry promptly took his own life. One down.

The next was not a husband. Jacob Denton could be classified as Louise's lover — and he was the first murder victim. By the time she hooked up with Denton, Louise had already married for the third time, the latest husband being Harold Peete. Louise quickly tired of Harold and left him in search of someone better, and that's when she found Denton.

He was a millionaire, fifty years old, and he lived all alone in a beautiful mansion in Los Angeles. It was a perfect set-up for Louise. She started out by being employed as his housekeeper, but that didn't last too long. Louise wasn't a young girl any longer, but she still had lots to offer a man. So, it was only a short time before Louise's housekeeping activities were extended to something a bit more intimate. However, the affair broke up when Louise was foolish enough to suggest that Denton legalize everything by marrying her. He laughed at her — and he laughed himself right into a neat little grave in his own cellar. Louise shot him very efficiently through the back of the head and buried him under a pile of fresh earth in a storage room in the cellar. Then she sealed up the room. Two down.

Louise then proceeded to add the crime of forgery to that of murder by forging Denton's name to some checks, and she lived quite comfortably off the proceeds. She even bluffed her way through visits to the house by a couple of suspicious relatives of Denton's; but, when things began to get too hot for her, Louise packed up and went back to her third husband, Harold Peete.

Harold welcomed her back without question, and they picked up their marriage where they had left it when Louise had gone off to be a housekeeper. Harold didn't know anything about what Louise had been doing in her absence — but he soon found out. It wasn't too long before Denton's body was discovered, and the police traced Louise through some trunks that she had shipped to herself at Harold's home.

The police came and arrested Louise. She was booked for the murder of Denton, tried, found guilty, and sentenced to life imprisonment. The blow was too much for Harold. He found he couldn't live without his Louise, so he stuck the barrel of a gun up against his head and pulled the trigger. Three down.

But Louise wasn't finished yet.

She spent the next eighteen years of her life in prison and then was paroled. She finally got another job as a housekeeper, this time with Mr. and Mrs. Arthur Logan, a very wealthy couple who had helped sponsor her parole. Louise was in her sixties by now, but that didn't stop her from acquiring a fourth husband soon after getting the job. The latest one was named Lee Judson, a quiet little man just a few years younger than Louise, and he came to live with her at the Logan house.

Things went along smoothly for a while, and then Louise decided to take over.

Mr. Logan had begun to show signs of mental weakness, so he didn't bother Louise at all. She concentrated on Mrs. Logan. Louise bided her time, and, once again, she used a gun and a shovel to get rid of her victim. She shot Mrs. Logan and then buried her under an avocado tree in the back yard. Four down.

Louise had no trouble covering up for this. She told her husband that Mrs. Logan had gone away on a trip, and Mr. Logan's mind had now deteriorated to the point where he didn't even realize what had happened. In fact, he was eventually committed to an insane asylum.

The Logans had lots of money, and with things the way they were now, Louise was able quite easily to latch on to most of the money for herself.

However, Louise was still on parole, and this meant that Mrs. Logan was supposed to send in a monthly report on Louise to the parole board. Naturally, she couldn't do it now, but Louise got around this small point by forging Mrs. Logan's signature to the reports.

Louise wasn't too good a forger, though, and the board soon caught on to the deception. An investigation was begun, and after that it was only a matter of police routine. Louise was arrested, tried, convicted, and this time sentenced to death — and executed.

Lee Judson, the hapless fourth husband, also found that life without Louise wasn't bearable. So, he made his way to an upper floor of an office building and jumped out into space. Five down.

There had been one other man in Louise's life before all the others — her very first husband, Bosley. But Bosley was a smart man, and he stayed alive. He had found he could live much more happily without Louise — and he had done something none of the others thought of doing. He divorced Louise.

During the day Freddy was an elevator operator. But at night he became, in a very strange way, a

Professional Man

A Novelette

BY

DAVID GOODIS

At five past five, the elevator operated by Freddy Lamb came to a stop on the street floor. Freddy smiled courteously to the departing passengers. As he said good-night to the office-weary faces of secretaries and bookkeepers and executives, his voice was soothing and cool-sweet, almost like a caress for the women and a pat on the shoulder for the men. People were very fond of

Freddy. He was always so pleasant, so polite and quietly cheerful. Of the five elevator-men in the Chambers Trust Building, Freddy Lamb was the favorite.

His appearance blended with his voice and manner. He was neat and clean and his hair was nicely trimmed. He had light brown hair parted on the side and brushed flat across his head. His eyes were the same color, focused level when he addressed you, but never too intent, never probing. He looked at you as though he liked and trusted you, no matter who you were. When you looked at him you felt mildly stimulated. He seemed much younger than his thirty-three years. There were no lines on his face, no sign of worry or sluggishness or dissipation. The trait that made him an ideal elevator-man was the fact that he never asked questions and never talked about himself.

At twenty past five, Freddy got the go-home sign from the starter, changed places with the night man, and walked down the corridor to the locker room. Taking off the uniform and putting on his street clothes, he yawned a few times. And while he was sitting on the bench and tying his shoelaces, he closed his eyes for a long moment, as though trying to catch a quick nap. His fingers fell away from the shoelaces and his shoulders drooped and he was in that position when the starter came in.

"Tired?" the starter asked.

"Just a little." Freddy looked up.

"Long day," the starter said. He was always saying that. As though each day was longer than any other.

Freddy finished with the shoelaces. He stood up and said, "You got the dollar-fifty?"

"What dollar-fifty?"

"The loan," Freddy said. He smiled off-handedly. "From last week. You ran short and needed dinner money. Remember?"

The starter's face was blank for a moment. Then he snapped his finger and nodded emphatically. "You're absolutely right," he declared. "I'm glad you reminded me."

He handed Freddy a dollar bill and two quarters. Freddy thanked him and said good-night and walked out. The starter stood there, lighting a cigarette and nodding to himself and thinking, *Nice guy, he waited a week before he asked me, and then he asked me so nice, he's really a nice guy.*

At precisely eight-ten, Freddy Lamb climbed out of the bathtub on the third floor of the uptown rooming house in which he lived. In his room, he opened a dresser drawer, took out silk underwear, silk socks, and a silk handkerchief. When he was fully dressed, he wore a pale grey roll-collar shirt that had cost fourteen dollars, a grey silk-gabardine suit costing ninety-seven fifty, and dark grey suede shoes that had set him back twenty-three ninety-five. He broke open a fresh pack of cigarettes and slipped them into a wafer-thin sterling silver case, and then he changed wrist watches. The one he'd been wearing was of mediocre quality and had a steel case. The one he wore now was fourteen karat white-gold. But both kept perfect time. He was very particular about the watches he bought. He wouldn't wear a watch that didn't keep absolutely perfect time.

The white-gold watch showed eight-twenty when Freddy walked out of the rooming house. He walked down Sixteenth to Ontario, then over to Broad and caught a cab. He gave the driver an address downtown. The cab's headlights merged with the flooded glare of southbound traffic. Freddy leaned back and lit a cigarette.

"Nice weather," the driver commented.

"Yes, it certainly is," Freddy said.

"I like it this time of year," the driver said. "It ain't too hot and it ain't too cold. It's just right." He glanced at the rear-view mirror and saw that his passenger was putting on a pair of dark glasses. He said, "You in show business?"

"No," Freddy said.

"What's the glasses for?"

Freddy didn't say anything.

"What's the glasses for?" the driver asked.

"The headlights hurt my eyes," Freddy said. He said it somewhat slowly, his tone indicating that he was rather tired and didn't feel like talking.

The driver shrugged and remained quiet for the rest of the ride. He brought the cab to a stop at the corner of Eleventh and Locust. The fare was a dollar twenty. Freddy gave him two dollars and told him to keep the change. As the cab drove away, Freddy walked west on Locust to Twelfth, walked south on Twelfth, then turned west again, moving through a narrow alley. There were no lights in the alley except for a rectangle of green neon far down toward the other end. The rectangle was a glowing frame for the neon wording, *Billy's Hut*. It was also a beckoning finger for that special type of citizen who was never happy unless he was being taken over in a clipjoint. They'd soon be flocking through the front entrance on Locust Street. But Freddy Lamb, moving toward the back entrance, had it checked in his mind that the place was empty now. The dial of his wrist watch showed eight-fifty-seven, and he knew it was too early for customers. He also knew that Billy Donofrio was sound asleep on a sofa in the back room used as a private office. He knew it because he'd been watching Donofrio for more than two weeks and he was well acquainted with Donofrio's nightly habits.

When Freddy was fifteen yards away from *Billy's Hut*, he reached into his inner jacket pocket and took out a pair of white cotton gloves. When he was five yards away, he came to a stop and stood motionless, listening. There was the sound of a record-player from some upstairs flat on the other side of the alley. From another upstairs flat there was the noise of lesbian voices saying, "You did," and "I didn't," and "You did, you did —"

He listened for other sounds and there were none. He let the tip of his tongue come out just a little to moisten the center of his lower lip. Then he took a few forward steps that brought him to a section of brick wall where the bricks were loose. He counted up from the bottom, the light from the green neon showing him the fourth brick, the fifth, the sixth and the seventh. The eighth brick was the one he wanted. He got a grip on its edges jutting away from the wall, pulled at it very slowly and carefully. Then he held it in one hand and his other hand reached into the empty space and made contact with the bone handle of a switchblade. It was a six-inch blade and he'd planted it there two nights ago.

He put the brick back in place and walked to the back door of *Billy's Hut*. Bending to the side to see through the window, he caught sight of Billy Donofrio on the sofa. Billy was flat on his back, one short leg dangling over the side of the sofa, one arm also dangling with fat fingers holding the stub of an unlit cigar. Billy was very short and very fat, and in his sleep he breathed as though it was a great effort. Billy was almost completely bald and what hair he had was more white than black. Billy was fifty-three years old and would never get to be fifty-four.

Freddy Lamb used a skeleton key to open the back door. He did it without sound. And then, without sound, he moved toward the sofa, his eyes focused on the crease of flesh between Billy's third chin and Billy's shirt collar. His arm went up and came down and the blade went into the crease, went in deep to cut the jugular vein, moved left, moved right, to widen the cut so that it was almost from ear to ear. Billy opened his eyes and tried to open his mouth but that was as far as he could take it. He tried to breathe and he couldn't breathe. He heard the voice of Freddy Lamb saying very softly, almost gently, "Good night, Billy." Then he heard Freddy's footsteps moving toward the door, and the door opening, and the footsteps walking out.

Billy didn't hear the door as it closed. By that time he was far away from hearing anything.

2.

On Freddy's wrist, the hands of the white-gold watch pointed to nine twenty-six. He stood on the sidwalk near the entrance of a nightclub called "Yellow Cat." The place was located in a low-rent area of South Philadelphia, and the neighboring structures were mostly tenements and garages and vacant lots heaped with rubbish. The club's exterior complied with the general trend; it was dingy and there was no paint on the wooden walls. But inside it was a different proposition. It was glittering and lavish, the drinks were expensive, and the floor show featured a first-rate orchestra and singers and dancers. It also featured a unique type of strip-tease entertainment, a quintet of young females who took off their clothes while they sat at your table. For a reasonable bonus they'd let you keep the brassiere or garter or whatnot for a souvenir.

The white-gold watch showed nine twenty-eight. Freddy decided to wait another two minutes. His appointment with the owner of "Yellow Cat" had been arranged for nine-thirty. He knew that Herman Charn was waiting anxiously for his arrival, but his personal theory of punctuality stipulated split-second precision, and since they'd made it for nine-thirty he'd see Herman at nine-thirty, not a moment earlier or later.

A taxi pulled up and a blonde stepped out. She paid the driver and walked toward Freddy and he said, "Hello, Pearl."

Pearl smiled at him. "Kiss me hello."

"Not here," he said.

"Later?"

He nodded. He looked her up and down. She was five-five and weighed one-ten and Nature had given her a body that caused men's eyes to bulge. Freddy's eyes didn't bulge, although he told himself she was something to see. He always enjoyed looking at her. He wondered if he still enjoyed the nights with her. He'd been sharing the nights with her for the past several months and it had reached the point where he wasn't seeing any other women and maybe he was missing out on something. For just a moment he gazed past Pearl, telling himself that she needed him more than he needed her, and knowing it wouldn't be easy to get off the hook.

Well, there wasn't any hurry. He hadn't seen anything else around that interested him. But he wished Pearl would let up on the clinging routine. Maybe he'd really go for her if she wasn't so hungry for him all the time.

Pearl stepped closer to him. The hunger showed in her eyes. She said, "Know what I did today? I took a walk in the park."

"You did?"

"Yeah," she said. "I went to Fairmount Park and took a long walk. All by myself."

"That's nice," he said. He wondered what she was getting at.

She said, "Let's do it together sometimes. Let's go for a walk in the park. It's something we ain't never done. All we do is drink and listen to jazz and find all sorts of ways to knock ourselves out."

He gave her a closer look. This was a former call-girl who'd done a stretch for prostitution, a longer stretch for selling cocaine, and had finally decided she'd done enough time and she might as well go legitimate. She'd learned the art of stripping off her clothes before an audience, and now at twenty-six she was earning a hundred-and-a-half a week. It was clean money, as far as the law was concerned, but maybe in her mind it wasn't clean enough. Maybe she was getting funny ideas, like this walk-in-the-park routine. Maybe she'd soon be thinking in terms of a cottage for two and a little lawn in front and shopping for a baby-carriage.

He wondered what she'd look like, wearing an apron and standing at a sink and washing dishes.

For some reason the thought disturbed him. He couldn't understand why it should disturb him. He heard her saying, "Can we do it, Freddy? Let's do it on Sunday. We'll go to Fairmount Park —"

"We'll talk about it," he cut in quickly. He glanced at his wrist watch. "See you after the show."

He hurried through the club entrance, went past the hat-check counter, past the tables and across the dance-floor and toward a door marked "Private." There was a button adjoining the door and he pressed the button one short, two longs, another short and then there was a buzzing sound. He opened the door and walked into the office. It was a large room and the color motif was yellow-and-grey. The walls and ceiling were gray and the thick carpet was pale yellow. The furniture was bright yellow. There was a short skinny man standing near the desk and his face was grey. Seated at the desk was a large man whose face was a mixture of yellow and grey.

Freddy closed the door behind him. He walked toward the desk. He nodded to the short skinny man and then he looked at the large man and said, "Hello, Herman."

Herman glanced at a clock on the desk. He said, "You're right on time."

"He's always on time," said the short skinny man.

Herman looked at Freddy Lamb and said, "You do it?"

Before Freddy could answer, the short skinny man said, "Sure he did it."

"Shut up, Ziggy," Herman said. He had a soft, sort of gooey voice, as though he spoke with a lot of marshmallow in his mouth. He wore a suit of very soft fabric, thick and fleecy, and his thick hands pressed softly on the desk-top. On the little finger of his left hand he wore a large star-emerald that radiated a soft green light. Everything about him was soft, except for his eyes. His eyes were iron.

"You do it?" he repeated softly.

Freddy nodded.

"Any trouble?" Herman asked.

"He never has trouble," Ziggy said.

Herman looked at Ziggy. "I told you to shut up." Then, very softly, "Come here, Ziggy."

Ziggy hesitated. He had a ferret

face that always looked sort of worried and now it looked very worried.

"Come here," Herman purred.

Ziggy approached the large man. Ziggy was blinking and swallowing hard. Herman reached out slowly and took hold of Ziggy's hand. Herman's thick fingers closed tightly on Ziggy's bony fingers, gave a yank and a twist and another yank. Ziggy moaned.

"When I tell you to shut up," Herman said, "you'll shut up." He smiled softly and paternally at Ziggy. "Right?"

"Right," Ziggy said. Then he moaned again. His fingers were free now and he looked down at them as an animal gazes sadly at its own crushed paws. He said, "They're all busted."

"They're not busted," Herman said. "They're damaged just enough to let you know your place. That's one thing you must never forget. Every man who works for me has to know his place." He was still smiling at Ziggy. "Right?"

"Right," Ziggy moaned.

Then Herman looked at Freddy Lamb and said, "Right?"

Freddy didn't say anything. He was looking at Ziggy's fingers. Then his gaze climbed to Ziggy's face. The lips quivered, as though Ziggy was trying to hold back sobs. Freddy remembered the time when nothing could hurt Ziggy, when Ziggy and himself were their own bosses and did their engineering on the waterfront. There were a lot of people on the waterfront who were willing to pay good money to have other people placed on stretchers or in caskets. In those days the rates had been fifteen dollars for a broken jaw, thirty for a fractured pelvis, and a hundred for the complete job. Ziggy handled the blackjack work and the bullet work and Freddy took care of such special functions as switchblade slicing, lye-in-the-eyes, and various powders and pills slipped into a glass of beer or wine or a cup of coffee. There were orders for all sorts of jobs in those days.

Fifteen months ago, he was thinking. And times had sure changed. The independent operator was swallowed up by the big combines. It was especially true in this line of business, which followed the theory that competition, no matter how small, was not good for the over-all picture. So the moment had come when he and Ziggy had been approached with an offer, and they knew they had to accept, there wasn't any choice, if they didn't accept they'd be erased. They didn't need to be told about that. They just knew. As much as they hated to do it, they had to do it. The proposition was handed to them on a Wednesday afternoon and that same night they went to work for Herman Charn.

He heard Herman saying, "I'm talking to you, Freddy."

"I hear you," he said.

"You sure?" Herman asked softly. "You sure you hear me?"

Freddy looked at Herman. He said quietly, "I'm on your payroll. I do what you tell me to do. I've done every job exactly the way you wanted it done. Can I do any more than that?"

"Yes," Herman said. His tone was matter-of-fact. He glanced at Ziggy and said, "From here on it's a private discussion. Me and Freddy. Take a walk."

Ziggy's mouth opened just a little. He didn't seem to understand the command. He'd always been included in all the business conferences, and now the look in his eyes was a mixture of puzzlement and injury.

Herman smiled at Ziggy. He pointed to the door. Ziggy bit hard on his lip and moved toward the door and opened it and walked out of the room.

For some moments it was quiet in the room and Freddy had a feeling it was too quiet. He sensed that Herman Charn was aiming something at him, something that had nothing to do with the ordinary run of business.

There was the creaking sound of leather as Herman leaned back in the desk-chair. He folded his big soft fingers across his big soft belly and said, "Sit down, Freddy. Sit down and make yourself comfortable."

Freddy pulled a chair toward the desk. He sat down. He looked at the face of Herman and for just a moment the face became a wall that moved toward him. He winced, his insides quivered. It was a strange sensation, he'd never had it before and he couldn't understand it. But then the moment was gone and he sat there relaxed, his features expressionless, as he waited for Herman to speak.

Herman said, "Want a drink?"

Freddy shook his head.

"Smoke?" Herman lifted the lid of an enamelled cigarette-box.

"I got my own," Freddy murmured. He reached into his pocket and took out the flat silver case.

"Smoke one of mine," Herman said. He paused to signify it wasn't a suggestion, it was an order. And then, as though Freddy was a guest rather than an employee, "These smokes are special-made. Come from Egypt. Cost a dime apiece."

Freddy took one. Herman flicked a table-lighter, applied the flame to Freddy's cigarette, lit one for himself, took a slow soft drag, and let the smoke come out of his nose. Herman waited until all the smoke was out, and then he said, "You didn't like what I did to Ziggy."

It was a flat statement that didn't ask for an answer. Freddy sipped at the cigarette, not looking at Herman.

"You didn't like it," Herman persisted softly. "You never like it when I let Ziggy know who's boss."

Freddy shrugged. "That's between you and Ziggy."

"No," Herman said. And then he spoke very slowly, with a pause between each word. "It isn't that way at all. I don't do it for Ziggy's benefit. He already knows who's top man around here."

Freddy didn't say anything. But he almost winced. And again his insides quivered.

Herman leaned forward. "Do you know who the top man is?"

"You," Freddy said.

Herman smiled. "Thanks, Freddy. Thanks for saying it." Then the smile vanished and Herman's eyes were hammerheads. "But I'm not sure you mean it."

Freddy took another sip from the Egyptian cigarette. It was strongly flavored tobacco but somehow he wasn't getting any taste from it.

Herman kept leaning forward. "I gotta be sure, Freddy," he said. "You been working for me more than a year. And just like you said, you do all the jobs exactly the way I want them done. You plan them perfect, do them perfect, it's always clean and neat from start to finish. I don't mind saying you're one of the best. I don't think I've ever seen a cooler head. You're as cool as they come, an icicle on wheels."

"That's plenty cool," Freddy murmured.

"It sure is," Herman said. He let the pause drift in again. Then, his lips scarcely moving, "Maybe it's too cool."

Freddy looked at the hammerhead eyes. He wondered what showed in his own eyes. He wondered what thoughts were burning under the cool surface of his own brain.

He heard Herman saying, "I've done a lot of thinking about you. A lot more than you'd ever imagine. You're a puzzler, and one thing I always like to do is play stud poker with a puzzler."

Freddy smiled dimly. "Want to play stud poker?"

"We're playing it now. Without cards." Herman gazed down at the desk-top. His right hand was on the desk-top and he flicked his wrist as though he was turning over the hole-card. His voice was very soft as he said, "I want you to break it up with Pearl."

Freddy heard himself saying, "All right, Herman."

It was as though Freddy hadn't spoken. Herman said, "I'm waiting, Freddy."

"Waiting for what?" He told the dim smile to stay on his lips. It stayed there. He murmured, "You tell me to give her up and I say all right. What more do you want me to say?"

"I want you to ask me why. Don't you want to know why?"

Freddy didn't reply. He still wore the dim smile and he was gazing past Herman's head.

"Come on, Freddy. I'm waiting to see your hole-card."

Freddy remained quiet.

"All right," Herman said. "I'll keep on showing you mine. I go for Pearl. I went for her the first time I laid eyes on her. That same night I took her home with me and she stayed over. She did what I wanted her to do but it didn't mean a thing to her, it was just like turning a trick. I thought it wouldn't bother me, once I have them in bed I can put them out of my mind. But this thing with Pearl, it's different. I've had her on my mind and it gets worse all the time and now it's gotten to the point where I have to do something about it. First thing I gotta do is clear the road."

"It's cleared," Freddy said. "I'll tell her tonight I'm not seeing her anymore."

"Just like that?" And Herman snapped his fingers.

"Yes," Freddy said. His fingers made the same sound. "Just like that."

Herman leaned back in the soft leather chair. He looked at the face of Freddy Lamb as though he was trying to solve a cryptogram. Finally he shook his head slowly, and then he gave a heavy sigh and he said, "All right, Freddy. That's all for now."

Freddy stood up. He started toward the door. Half-way across the room he stopped and turned and said, "You promised me a bonus for the Donofrio job."

"This is Monday," Herman said. "I hand out the pay on Friday."

"You said I'd be paid right off."

"Did I?" Herman smiled softly.

"Yes," Freddy said. "You said the deal on Donofrio was something special and the customer was paying fifteen hundred. You told me there was five hundred in it for me and I'd get the bonus the same night I did the job."

Herman opened a desk-drawer and took out a thick roll of bills.

"Can I have it in tens and twenties?" Freddy asked.

Herman lifted his eyebrows. "Why the small change?"

"I'm an elevator man," Freddy said. "The bank would wonder what I was doing with fifties."

"You're right," Herman said. He counted off the five hundred in tens and twenties, and handed the money to Freddy. He leaned back in the chair and watched Freddy folding the bills and pocketing them and walking out of the room. When the door was closed, Herman said aloud to himself, "Don't try to figure him out, he's all ice and no soul, strictly a professional."

3.

The white-gold watch showed eleven thirty-five. Freddy sat at a table watching the floor show and drinking from a tall glass of gin-and-ginger ale. The *Yellow Cat* was crowded now and Freddy wore the dark glasses and his table was in a darkly shadowed section of the room. He sat there with Ziggy and some other men who worked for Herman. There was Dino, who did his jobs at long-range and always used a rifle. There was Shikey, six-foot-six and weighing three hundred pounds, an expert at bone-cracking, gouging, and the removing of teeth. There was Riley, another bone-cracker and strangling specialist.

A tall pretty boy stood in front of the orchestra, clutching the mike as though it was the only support he had in the world. He sang with an ache in his voice, begging someone to "— please understand." The audience liked it and he sang it again. Then two colored tap-dancers came out and worked themselves into a sweat and were gasping for breath as they finished the act. The M.C. walked on and motioned the orchestra to quiet down and grinned at ringside faces as he said, "Ready for dessert?"

"Yeah," a man shouted from ringside. "Let's have the dessert."

"All right," the M.C. said. He cupped his hands to his mouth and called off-stage, "Bring it out, we're all starved for that sweetmeat."

The orchestra went into medium tempo, the lights changed from glaring yellow to a soft violet. And then they came out, seven girls wearing horn-rimmed glasses and ultra-conservative costumes. They walked primly, and altogether they resembled the stiff-necked females in a cartoon lampooning the W.C.T.U. It got a big laugh from the audience, and there was some appreciative applause. The young ladies formed a line and slowly waved black parasols as they sang, "— Father, oh father, come home with me now." But then it became, "— Daddy, oh daddy, come home with me now." And as they emphasized the daddy angle, they broke up the line and discarded the parasols and took off their ankle-length dark-blue coats. Then, their fingers loosening the buttons of dark-blue dresses, they moved separately toward the ringside tables. The patrons in the back stood up to get a better look and in the balcony the lenses of seven lamps were focused on seven young women getting undressed.

Dino, who had a footwear fetish, said loudly, "I'll pay forty for a high-heeled shoe."

One of the girls took off her shoe and flung it toward Freddy's table. Shikey caught it and handed it to Dino. A waiter came over and Dino handed him four tens and he took the money to the girl. Riley looked puzzledly at Dino and said, "Whatcha gonna do with a high-heeled shoe?" And Shikey said, "He boils 'em and eats 'em." But Ziggy had another theory. "He bangs the heel against his head," Ziggy said. "That's the way he gets his kicks." Dino sat there gazing lovingly at the shoe in his hand while his other hand caressed the kidskin surface. Then gradually his eyes closed and he murmured, "This is nice, this is so nice."

Riley was watching Dino and saying, "I don't get it."

Ziggy shrugged philosophically. "Some things," he said, "just can't be understood."

"You're so right." It was Freddy

talking. He didn't know his lips were making sound. He was looking across the tables at Pearl. She sat with some ringsiders and already she'd taken off considerable clothing, she was half-naked. On her face there was a detached look and her hands moved mechanically as she unbuttoned the buttons and unzipped the zippers. There were three men sitting with her and their eyes feasted on her, they had their mouths open in a sort of mingled fascination and worship. At nearby tables the other strippers were performing but they weren't getting undivided attention. Most of the men were watching Pearl. One of them offered a hundred dollars for her stocking. She took off the stocking and let it dangle from her fingers. In a semi-whisper she asked if there were any higher bids. Freddy told himself that she wasn't happy doing what she was doing. Again he could hear her plaintive voice as she asked him to take her for a walk in the park. Suddenly he knew that he'd like that very much. He wanted to see the sun shining on her hair, instead of the night-club lights. He heard himself saying aloud, "Five hundred."

He didn't shout it, but at the ringside tables they all heard it, and for a moment there was stunned silence. At his own table the silence was very thick. He could feel the pressure of it, and the moment seemed to have substance, something on the order of iron wheels going around and around, making no sound and getting nowhere.

Some things just can't be understood, he thought. He was taking the tens and twenties from his jacket pocket. The five hundred seemed to prove the truth of Ziggy's vague philosophy. Freddy got up from his chair and moved toward an empty table behind some potted ferns adjacent to the orchestra-stand. He sat down and placed green money on a yellow tablecloth. He wasn't looking at Pearl as she approached the table. From ringside an awed voice was saying, "For one silk stocking she gets half a grand —"

She seated herself at the table. He shoved the money toward her. He said, "There's your cash. Let's have the stocking."

"This a gag?" she asked quietly. Her eyes were somewhat sullen. There was some laughter from the table where Ziggy and the others were seated; they now had the notion it was some sort of joke.

Freddy said, "Take off the stocking."

She looked at the pile of tens and twenties. She said, "Whatcha want the stocking for?"

"Souvenir," he said.

It was the tone of his voice that did it. Her face paled. She started to shake her head very slowly, as though she couldn't believe him.

"Yes," he said, with just the trace of a sigh. "It's all over, Pearl. It's the end of the line."

She went on shaking her head. She couldn't talk.

He said, "I'll hang the stocking in my bedroom."

She was biting her lip. "It's a long time till Christmas."

"For some people it's never Christmas."

"Freddy —" She leaned toward him. "What's it all about? Why're you doing this?"

He shrugged. He didn't say anything.

Her eyes were getting wet. "You won't even give me a reason?"

All he gave her was a cool smile. Then his head was turned and he saw the faces at Ziggy's table and then he focused on the face of the large man who stood behind the table. He saw the iron in the eyes of Herman Charn. He told himself he was doing what Herman had told him to do. And just then he felt the quiver in his insides. It was mostly in his spine, as though his spine was gradually turning to jelly.

He spoke to himself without sound. He said, *No, it isn't that, it can't be that.*

Pearl was saying, "All right, Freddy, if that's the way it is."

He nodded very slowly.

Pearl bent over and took the stocking off her leg. She placed the stocking on the table. She picked up the five hundred, counted it off to make sure it was all there.

Then she stood up and said, "No charge, mister. I'd rather keep the memories."

She put the tens and twenties on the tablecloth and walked away. Freddy glanced off to the side and saw a soft smile on the face of Herman Charn.

4.

The floor-show was ended and Freddy was still sitting there at the table. There was a bottle of bourbon in front of him. It had been there for less than twenty minutes and already it was half-empty. There was also a pitcher of ice-water and the pitcher was full. He didn't need a chaser because he couldn't taste the whiskey. He was drinking the whiskey from the water-glass.

A voice said, "Freddy —"

And then a hand tugged at his arm. He looked up and saw Ziggy sitting beside him.

He smiled at Ziggy. He motioned toward the bottle and shot-glass and said, "Have a drink."

Ziggy shrugged. "I might as well while I got the chance. At the rate you're going, that bottle'll soon be empty."

"It's very good bourbon," Freddy said.

"Yeah?" Ziggy was pouring a glass for himself. He swished the liquor into his mouth. Then, looking closely at Freddy, "You don't care whether it's good or not. You'd be gulping it if it was shoe-polish."

Freddy was staring at the tablecloth. "Let's go somewhere and drink some shoe-polish."

Ziggy tugged again at Freddy's arm. He said, "Come out of it."

"Come out of what?"

"The clouds," Ziggy said. "You're in the clouds."

"It's nice in the clouds," Freddy said. "I'm up here having a dandy time. I'm floating."

"Floating? You're drowning." Ziggy pulled urgently at his arm, to get his hand away from a water-glass filled with whiskey. "You're not a drinker, Freddy. What do you want to do, drink yourself into a hospital?"

Freddy grinned. He aimed the grin at nothing in particular. For some moments he sat there motionless. Then he reached into his jacket pocket and took out the silk stocking. He showed it to Ziggy and said, "Look what I got."

"Yeah," Ziggy said. "I seen her give it to you. What's the score on that routine?"

"No score," Freddy said. He went on grinning. "It's a funny way to end a game. Nothing on the scoreboard. Nothing at all."

Ziggy frowned. "You trying to tell me something?"

Freddy looked at the whiskey in the water-glass. He said, "I packed her in."

"No," Ziggy said. His tone was incredulous. "Not Pearl. Not that pigeon. That ain't no ordinary merchandise. You wouldn't walk out on Pearl unless you had a very special reason."

"It was special, all right."

"Tell me about it, Freddy." There was something plaintive in Ziggy's voice, a certain feeling for Freddy that he couldn't put into words. The closest he could get to it was, "After all, I'm on your side, ain't I?"

"No," Freddy said. The grin was slowly fading. "You're on Herman's side." He gazed past Ziggy's head. "We're all on Herman's side."

"Herman? What's he got to do with it?"

"Everything," Freddy said. "Herman's the boss, remember?" He looked at the swollen fingers of Ziggy's right hand. "Herman wants something done, it's got to be done. He gave me orders to break with Pearl. He's the employer and I'm the hired man, so I did what I had to do. I carried out his orders."

Ziggy was quiet for some moments. Then, very quietly, "Well, it figures he wants her for himself. But it don't seem right. It just ain't fair."

"Don't make me laugh," Freddy said. "Who the hell are we to say what's fair?"

"We're human, aren't we?"

"No," Freddy said. He gazed past Ziggy's head. "I don't know what we are. But I know one thing, we're not human. We can't afford to be human, not in this line of business."

Ziggy didn't get it. It was just a little too deep for him. All he could say was, "You getting funny ideas?"

"I'm not reaching for them, they're just coming to me."

"Take another drink." Ziggy said.

"I'd rather have the laughs." Freddy showed the grin again. "It's really comical, you know? Especially this thing with Pearl. I was thinking of calling it quits anyway. You know how it is with me, Ziggy. I never like to be tied down to one skirt. But tonight Pearl said something that spun me around. We were talking outside the club and she brought it in out of left field. She asked me to take her for a walk in the park."

Ziggy blinked a few times. "What?"

"A walk in the park," Freddy said.

"What for?" Ziggy wanted to know. "She gettin' square all of a sudden? She wanna go around picking flowers?"

"I don't know," Freddy said. "All she said was, it's very nice in Fairmount Park. She asked me to take her there and we'd be together in the park, just taking a walk."

Ziggy pointed to the glass. "You better take that drink."

Freddy reached for the glass. But someone else's hand was there first. He saw the thick soft fingers, the soft green glow of the star-emerald. As the glass of whiskey was shoved out of his reach, he looked up and saw the soft smile on the face of Herman Charn.

"Too much liquor is bad for the kidneys," Herman said. He bent down lower to peer at Freddy's eyes. "You look knocked-out, Freddy. There's a soft couch in the office. Go in there and lie down for awhile."

Freddy got up from the chair. He was somewhat unsteady on his feet. Herman took his arm and helped him make it down the aisle past the tables to the door of the office. He could feel the pressure of Herman's hand on his arm. It was very soft pressure but somehow it felt like a clamp of iron biting into his flesh.

Herman opened the office-door and guided him toward the couch. He fell onto the couch, sent an idiotic grin toward the ceiling, then closed his eyes and went to sleep.

5.

He slept until four-forty in the morning. The sound that woke him up was a scream.

At first it was all blurred, there was too much whiskey-fog in his brain, he had no idea where he was or what was happening. He pushed his knuckles against his eyes. Then, sitting up, he focused on the faces in the room. He saw Shikey and Riley and they had girls sitting in their laps. They were on the other couch at the opposite side of the room. He saw Dino standing near the couch with his arm around the waist of a slim brunette. Then he glanced toward the door and he saw Ziggy. That made seven faces for him to look at. He told himself to keep looking at them. If he concentrated on that, maybe he wouldn't hear the screaming.

But he heard it. The scream was an animal sound and yet he recognized the voice. It came from near the desk and he turned his head very slowly, telling himself he didn't want to look but knowing he had to look.

He saw Pearl kneeling on the floor. Herman stood behind her. With one hand he was twisting her arm up high between her shoulder blades. His other hand was on her head and he was pulling her hair so that her face was drawn back, her throat stretched.

Herman spoke very softly. "You make me very unhappy, Pearl. I don't like to be unhappy."

Then Herman gave her arm another upward twist and pulled tighter on her hair and she screamed again.

The girl in Shikey's lap gave Pearl a scornful look and said, "You're a damn fool."

"In spades." It came from the stripper who nestled against Riley. "All he wants her to do is kiss him like she means it."

Freddy told himself to get up and walk out of the room. He lifted himself from the couch and took a few steps toward the door and heard Herman saying, "Not yet, Freddy. I'll tell you when to go."

He went back to the couch and sat down.

Herman said, "Be sensible, Pearl. Why can't you be sensible?"

Pearl opened her mouth to scream again. But no sound came out. There was too much pain and it was choking her.

The brunette who stood with Dino was saying, "It's a waste of time, Herman. She can't give you what she hasn't got. She just don't have it for you, Herman."

"She'll have it for him," Dino said. "Before he's finished, he'll have her crawling on her belly."

Herman looked at Dino. "No," he said. "She won't do that. I wouldn't let her do that." He cast a downward glance at Pearl. His lips shaped a soft smile. There was something tender in the smile and in his voice. "Pearl, tell me something. Why don't you want me?"

He gave her a chance to reply, his fingers slackening the grip on her wrist and her hair. She groaned a few times, and then she said, "You got my body, Herman. You can have my body anytime you want it."

"That isn't enough," Herman said. "I want you all the way, a hundred percent. It's got to be like that, Pearl. You're in me so deep it just can't take any other route. It's gotta be you and me from here on in, you gotta need me just as much as I need you."

"But Herman —" She gave a dry sob. "I can't lie to you. I just don't feel that way."

"You're gonna feel that way," Herman said.

"No." Pearl sobbed again. "No. No."

"Why not?" He was pulling her hair again, twisting her arm. But it seemed he was suffering more than Pearl. The pain wracked his pleading voice. "Why can't you feel something for me?"

Her reply was made without sound. She managed to turn her head just a little, toward the couch. And everyone in the room saw her looking at Freddy.

Herman's face became very pale. His features tightened and twisted and it seemed he was about to burst into tears. He stared up at the ceiling.

Herman shivered. His body shook spasmodically, as though he stood on a vibrating platform. Then all at once the tormented look faded from his eyes, the iron came into his eyes, and the soft smile came onto his lips. He released Pearl, turned away from her, went to the desk and opened the cigarette-box. It was very quiet in the room while Herman stood there lighting the cigarette. He took a slow, easy drag and then he said quietly, "All right, Pearl, you can go home now."

She started to get up from the floor. The brunette came over and helped her up.

"I'll call a cab for you," Herman said. He reached for the telephone and put in the call. As he lowered the phone, he was looking at Pearl and saying, "You want to go home alone?"

Pearl didn't say anything. Her head was lowered and she was leaning against the shoulder of the brunette.

Herman said, "You want Freddy to take you home?"

Pearl raised her head just a little and looked at the face of Freddy Lamb.

Herman laughed softly. "All right," he said. "Freddy'll take you home."

Freddy winced. He sat there staring at the carpet.

Herman told the brunette to fix a drink for Pearl. He said, "Take her to the bar and give her anything she wants." He motioned to the other girls and they got up from the laps of Shikey and Riley. Then all the girls walked out of the room. Herman was quiet for some moments, taking slow drags at the cigarette and looking at the door. Then gradually his head turned and he looked at Freddy. He said, "You're slated, Freddy."

Freddy went on staring at the carpet.

"You're gonna bump her," Herman said.

Freddy closed his eyes.

"Take her somewhere and bump her and bury her," Herman said.

Shikey and Riley looked at each other. Dino had his mouth open and he was staring at Herman. Standing next to the door, Ziggy had his eyes glued to Freddy's face.

"She goes," Herman said. And then, speaking aloud to himself, "She goes because she gives me grief." He hit his hand against his chest. "She hits me here, where I live. Hits me too hard. Hurts me. I don't appreciate getting hurt.

Especially here." Again his hand thumped his chest. He said, "You'll do it, Freddy. You'll see to it that I get rid of the hurt."

"Let me do it," Ziggy said.

Herman shook his head. He pointed a finger at Freddy. His finger jabbed empty air, and he said, "Freddy does it. Freddy."

Ziggy opened his mouth, tried to close it, couldn't close it, and blurted, "Why take it out on him?"

"That's a stupid question," Herman said mildly. "I'm not taking it out on anybody. I'm giving the job to Freddy because I know he's dependable. I can always depend on Freddy."

Ziggy made a final frantic try. "Please, Herman," he said. "Please don't make him do it."

Herman didn't bother to reply. All he did was give Ziggy a slow appraising look up and down. It was like a soundless warning to Ziggy, letting him know he was walking on thin ice and the ice would crack if he opened his mouth again.

Then Herman turned to Freddy and said, "Where's your blade?"

"Stashed," Freddy said. He was still staring at the carpet.

Herman opened a desk-drawer. He took out a black-handled switchblade. "Use this," he said, coming toward the couch. He handed the knife to Freddy. "Give it a try," he said.

Freddy pressed the button. The blade flicked out. It glimmered blue-white. He pushed the blade into the handle and tried the button again. He went on trying the button and watching the flash of the blade. It was quiet in the room as the blade went in and out, in and out. Then from the street there was the sound of a horn. Herman said, "That's the taxi." Freddy nodded and got up from the sofa and walked out of the room. As he moved toward the girls who stood at the cocktail bar, he could feel the weight of the knife in the inner pocket of his jacket. He was looking at Pearl and saying, "Come on, let's go," and as he said it, the blade seemed to come out of the knife and slice into his own flesh.

6.

The taxi was cruising north on Sixteenth Street. On Freddy's wrist the white-gold watch said five-twenty. He was watching the parade of unlit windows along the dark street. Pearl was saying something but he didn't hear. She spoke just a bit louder and he turned and looked at her. He smiled and murmured, "Sorry, I wasn't listening."

"Can't you sit closer?"

He moved closer to her. A mixture of moonlight and streetlamp glow came pouring into the back-seat of the taxi and illuminated her face. He saw something in her eyes that caused him to blink several times.

She noticed the way he was blinking, and she said, "What's the matter?"

He didn't answer. He tried to stop blinking and he couldn't stop.

"Hangover?" Pearl asked.

"No," he said. "I feel all right now. I feel fine."

For some moments she didn't say anything. She was rubbing her sore arm. She tried to stretch it, winced and gasped with pain, and said, "Oh Jesus, it hurts. It really hurts. Maybe it's broken."

"Let me feel it," he said. He put his hand on her arm. He ran his fingers down from above her elbow to her wrist. "It isn't broken," he murmured. "Just a little swollen, that's all. Sprained some ligaments."

She smiled at him. "The hurt goes away when you touch it."

He tried not to look at her, but something fastened his eyes to her face. He kept his hand on her arm. He heard himself saying, "I feel sorry for Herman. If he could see you now, I mean if you'd look at him like you're looking at me —"

"Freddy," she said. "Freddy." Then she leaned toward him. She rested her head on his shoulder.

Then somehow everything was quiet and still and he didn't hear the noise of the taxi's engine, he didn't feel the bumps as the wheels hit the ruts in the cobblestoned surface of Sixteenth Street. But suddenly there was a deep rut and the taxi gave a lurch. He looked up and heard the driver cursing the city engineers. "Goddamit," the driver said. "They got a deal with the tire companies."

Freddy stared past the driver's head, his eyes aimed through the windshield to see the wide intersection where Sixteenth Street met the Parkway. The Parkway was a six-laned drive slanting to the left of the downtown area, going away from the concrete of Philadelphia skyscrapers and pointing toward the green of Fairmount Park.

"Turn left," Freddy said.

They were approaching the intersection, and the driver gave a backward glance. "Left?" the driver asked. "That takes us outta the way. You gave me an address on Seventeenth near Lehigh. We gotta hit it from Sixteenth —"

"I know," Freddy said quietly. "But turn left anyway."

The driver shrugged. "You're the captain." He beat the yellow of a traffic-light and the taxi made a left turn onto the Parkway.

Pearl said, "What's this, Freddy? Where're we going?"

"In the park." He wasn't looking at her. "We're gonna do what you said we should do. We're gonna take a walk in the park."

"For real?" Her eyes were lit up. She shook her head, as though she could scarcely believe what he'd just said.

"We'll take a nice walk," he murmured. "Just the two of us. The way you wanted it."

"Oh," she breathed. "Oh, Freddy —"

The driver shrugged again. The taxi went past the big monuments and fountains of Logan Circle, past the Rodin Museum and the Art Museum and onto River Drive. For a mile or so they stayed on the highway bordering the moonlit water of the river and then without being told the driver made a turn off the highway, made a series of turns that took them deep into the park. They came to a section where there were no lights, no movement, no sound except the autumn wind drifting through the trees and bushes and tall grass and flowers.

"Stop here," Freddy said.

The taxi came to a stop. They got out and he paid the driver. The driver gave him a queer look and said, "You sure picked a lonely spot."

Freddy looked at the cabman. He didn't say anything.

The driver said, "You're at least three miles off the highway. It's gonna be a problem getting a ride home."

"Is it your problem?" Freddy asked gently.

"Well, no —"

"Then don't worry about it," Freddy said. He smiled amiably. The driver threw a glance at the blonde, smiled, and told himself that the man might have the right idea, after all. With an item like that, any man would want complete privacy. He thought of the bony, buck-toothed woman who waited for him at home, crinkled his face in a distasteful grimace, put the car in gear and drove away.

"Ain't it nice?" Pearl said. "Ain't it wonderful?"

They were walking through a glade where the moonlight showed the autumn colors of fallen leaves. The night air was fragrant with the blended aromas of wild flowers. He had his arm around her shoulder and he was leading her toward a narrow lane sloping downward through the trees.

She laughed lightly, happily. "It's like as if you know the place. As if you've been here before."

"No," he said. "I've never been here before."

There was the tinkling sound of a nearby brook. A bird chirped in the bushes. Another bird sang a tender reply.

"Listen," Pearl murmured. "Listen to them."

He listened to the singing of the birds. Now he was guiding Pearl down along the slope and seeing the way it levelled at the bottom and then went up again on all sides. It was a tiny valley down there, with the brook running along the edge. He told himself it would happen when they reached the bottom.

He heard Pearl saying, "Wouldn't it be nice if we could stay here?"

He looked at her. "Stay here?"

"Yes," she said. "If we could live here for the rest of our lives. Just be here, away from everything —"

"We'd get lonesome."

"No we wouldn't," she said. "We'd always have company. I'd have you and you'd have me."

They were nearing the bottom of the slope. It was sort of steep now and they had to move slowly. All at once she stumbled and pitched forward and he caught her before she could fall on her face. He steadied her, smiled at her and said, "Okay?"

She nodded. She stood very close to him and gazed into his eyes and said, "You wouldn't let me fall, would you?"

The smile faded. He stared past her. "Not if I could help it."

"I know," she said. "You don't have to tell me."

He went on staring past her. "Tell you what?"

"The situation." She spoke softly, almost in a whisper. "I got it figured, Freddy. It's so easy to figure."

He wanted to close his eyes. He couldn't understand why he wanted to close his eyes.

He heard her saying, "I know why you packed me in tonight. Orders from Herman."

"That's right." He said it automatically, as though the mention of the name was the shifting of a gear.

"And another thing," she said. "I know why you brought me here." There was a pause, and then, very softly, "Herman."

He nodded.

She started to cry. It was quiet weeping and contained no fear, no hysteria. It was the weeping of farewell. She was crying because she was sad. Then, very slowly, she took the few remaining steps going down to the bottom of the slope. He stood there and watched her as she faced about to look up at him.

He walked down to where she stood, smiling at her and trying to pretend his hand was not on the switchblade in his pocket. He tried to make himself believe he wasn't going to do it, but he knew that wasn't true. He'd been slated for this job. The combine had him listed as a top-rated operator, one of the best in the business. He'd expended a lot of effort to attain that reputation, to be known as the grade-A expert who'd never muffed an assignment.

He begged himself to stop. He couldn't stop. The knife was open in his hand and his arm flashed out and sideways with the blade sliding in neatly and precisely, cutting the flesh of her throat. She went down very slowly, tried to cough, made a few gurgling sounds, and then rolled over on her back and died, looking up at him.

For a long time he stared at her face. There was no expression on her features now. At first he didn't feel anything, and then he realized she was dead, and he had killed her.

He tried to tell himself there was nothing else he could have done, but even though that was true it didn't do any good. He took his glance away from her face and looked down at the white-gold watch to check the hour and the minute, automatically. But somehow the dial was blurred, as though the hands were spinning like tiny propellers. He had the weird feeling that the watch was showing Time travelling backward, so that he found himself checking it in terms of years and decades. He went all the way back to the day when he was eleven years old and they took him to reform school.

In reform school he was taught a lot of things. The thing he learned best was the way to use a knife. The knife became his profession. But somewhere along the line he caught onto the idea of holding a daytime job to cover his night-time activities. He worked in stockrooms and he did some window-cleaning and drove a truck for a fruit-dealer. And finally he became an elevator operator and that was the job he liked best. He'd never realized why he liked it so much but he realized now. He knew that the elevator was nothing more than a moving cell, that the only place for him was a cell. The passengers were just a lot of friendly visitors walking in and out, saying "Good morning, Freddy," and "Good night, Freddy," and they were such nice people. Just the thought of them brought a tender smile to his lips.

Then he realized he was smiling down at her. He sensed a faint glow coming from somewhere, lighting her face. For an instant he had no idea what it was. Then he realized it came from the sky. It was the first signal of approaching sunrise.

The white-gold watch showed five fifty-three. Freddy Lamb told himself to get moving. For some reason he couldn't move. He was looking down at the dead girl. His hand was still clenched about the switchblade, and as he tried to relax it he almost dropped the knife. He looked down at it.

The combine was a cell, too, he told himself. The combine was an elevator from which he could never escape. It was going steadily downward and there were no stops until the end. There was no way to get out.

Herman had made him kill the girl. Herman would make him do other things. And there was no getting away from that. If he killed Herman there would be someone else.

The elevator was carrying Freddy steadily downward. Already, he had left Pearl somewhere far above him. He realized it all at once, and an unreasoning terror filled him.

Freddy looked at the white-gold watch again. A minute had passed, and he knew suddenly that he was slated to do a job on someone in exactly three minutes now. The minutes passed and he stood there alone.

At precisely five fifty-seven he said goodbye to his profession and plunged the blade into his heart.

Summer is a Bad Time

He'd promised never to lay a hand on her in anger. That was what made his revenge so terrible.

BY SAM S. TAYLOR

The blonde ran another tissue across her perspiring face and neck, then rolled down the coupe's window an inch, pushing out the crumpled paper. She shut it immediately, but the brief intake of Arizona desert air was like a branding iron against her cheek. She said fretfully, "For God's sake, Walt, will you step on it? I can't take much more of this."

"Can't risk it, Della. Not in this kind of heat. We'd blow a couple of tires, for sure." He had a lean thoughtful face, and he was about thirty. The quiet brown eyes had narrowed as he tried to accommodate his vision to the molten glare, leaping at him from the highway that stretched like an infinite yardstick to the Painted Rock Mountains, shimmering far to the east.

His wife's head fell back wearily. A bare arm drooped toward the box of tissues at her side. "How much longer before we stop somewhere where I can cool off?"

"Nothing worth mentioning this side of Gila Bend. Guess we can make that by one-thirty."

"One-thirty! Oh, God —" It tapered off into a moan at the prospect of more than another hour in this sealed bake oven. Her lids came down like a final curtain. "I should have had my head examined for coming along on one of your damned business trips."

"August's the worst time to come down here. I tried to tell you that, Della."

Anger snapped open her eyes. "All right, all right. So you told me. You don't have to rub it in. I just wanted to get away from that house for a change. How'd I know it was going to be like this?"

A car was approaching. The first in many miles. Walt said, "I'm sorry, Della. I used to go to school around Yuma. I'm used to this 125-degree stuff. But I knew it would be too much for you. I tried to warn —"

"Aw, shut up. Bad enough I have to be suffering this way, without your arguing . . . arguing." She jerked a fresh tissue from the box, dabbing at her skin. Delicate camelia-like skin that seemed strangely out of place in this sun-tortured waste land they were driving through.

Except for a minute tug at one corner of his mouth, the man showed no reaction. His steady glance remained on the approaching car. There was a slight body sway to the coupe when the other whipped by, then there was nothing to distinguish the surrounding vastness from a burned out planet, save the unswerving ribbon of dark gray pavement that pointed ahead like the finger of death.

After a while, she said, "I still don't see why we couldn't have waited until after dark to start out for Tucson, instead of driving through this hell."

"Just wouldn't have worked. The buyer for Maxwell Drug Company is flying east first thing tomorrow. He told me over the phone he'd wait around for me this evening. You know how big they are. You've been unhappy over the money you have to spend, Della. Well, you wouldn't want me to lose out on all that commission —."

"Okay, skip it, my big generous provider." A few more moments of silence, then there was a curious shift in her voice. "You know . . . I'm just beginning to wonder."

"What, Della?"

"Whether you didn't purposely arrange this stinking daytime trip just to make me suffer. Like you were trying to hurt me for something."

"Any reason why I should, dear?"

She studied his profile, with a quick sidelong glance. "No. No, not a one."

There was a fractional smile. He said in that quiet way, "Well, that should answer your question. Besides, you seem to forget something."

"Meaning?"

"I once promised you I'd never lay a finger on you in anger. No matter what you did."

Head lolling against the seat, she laughed throatily. "Yes. And knowing you the way I do, Walt, I really believe you." The overtone was scornful. "I really believe you wouldn't lay a finger on anybody or anything, no matter what."

The man's half-smile etched a little deeper. He didn't reply. Five more oppressive miles ticked off before he looked at her. Sleep was finally giving Della relief, and her unbuttoned blouse took on dimension with each rhythmic thrust of her luxurious breasts. Their creamy roundness was only partially screened. Walt's eyes inched past them, drifting down the sweep of her provocative body. For an instant he had that feeling again. The one that started a prairie fire in his stomach. Like that first night, eighteen months ago, at Smitty's Place, on Western Avenue. After finishing her vocal stint, she'd come over to the bar and Smitty had introduced them. Eighteen months ago. That instant of feeling was consumed now, leaving a thin bitter line across his mouth. He turned back to the deserted road, and his fingers dug into the wheel.

Last night that supple body had been caressed by another man.

The highway was an unreeling film strip of grating memory now. Earlier scenes lost themselves in quick dissolves, but the more recent came into sharp focus and held. There was that early evening last month when he got back from Santa Barbara with some juicy orders to show for the outing, which shouldn't make Mercury Drug Distributors at all unhappy that they'd added the town to his regular route. Walt whistled as he parked the Chevy in the alley garage, then lifted the little gift package from the seat and slipped it into his pocket.

Crossing over the rear lawn to his modest home, he caught the shrill blend of childish screams and laughter that rose from familiar backyards down the length of the tract. A young woman with the spread hips of advancing pregnancy called a greeting from the other side of the chain-link fence. She was removing diapers from a line. He glanced at them wistfully. There were times, it seemed to Walt, when diapers were strung out on neighboring lines as far as the eye could see. Like proud pennants during a fleet review. Every backyard but his. Well, there are some things you just can't rush. Della was still young. Guess you couldn't blame her in a way, with a figure like hers. He looked up at the two lone items on his own line. A sheer nylon step-in, with matching bra.

Opening the door of the service porch, he heard another scream. This time it wasn't a youngster's. He rushed to the bedroom. Della was standing in the middle of the bed. Both Della and the bed were still unmade. The long platinum-tipped nail of a thumb was clenched between gritted teeth. Her other hand pointed fearfully at a pillow she had apparently shoved to the floor.

He asked anxiously, "What's the matter, Della?"

"Don't you see it? A tarantula!"

He went over quickly and examined the inanimate black object lying on the pillow. He started a reassuring smile. "It can't hurt you, honey. Just a beetle. A real big one, but just —"

"Well, step on it! You know how I hate those horrible things." When his glance shifted unhurriedly about the room, the woman snapped again, "What are you horsing around for? Get rid of it!"

"I will, honey. Just a second." He went to the dresser, lifted a magazine, then brought it back to the pillow. Dropping to one knee Walt tried to prod the large insect into scrambling onto the magazine. The beetle refused to cooperate.

Exasperation shot the woman's voice up. "Christ' sake, Walt, will you kill that damn thing, and stop driving me crazy!"

"What's the use? It's perfectly harmless." He finally coaxed the beetle into activity. "Now we got him. I'll toss him back outside." He straightened and started to raise the window.

Della was sitting on the edge of the bed now. Disgust quirked her mouth. "Still the conscientious objector, aren't you? Even over bugs."

For a fleeting instant Walt's back was a study in arrested motion, then he resumed opening the window. He flipped the insect to the ground outside. He said quietly, without turning, "I thought I'd explained all that. I just don't believe in killing things that don't need killing."

There was a derisive little laugh, then she reached for a stocking on the floor and slipped it over a leg. "You're quite a guy, Walt. Quite a guy."

He went into the bathroom and spent some time under the shower. It helped to wash away the hurt of her earlier remark. Later, when she was in the kitchen emptying a canned stew into a saucepan, Walt came in with the gift package. "Almost forgot. Here's a little something I picked up for you today in Santa Barbara."

That produced her first unhostile smile. "Well, well. You really can surprise me. Open it, huh, Pidgie? My hands are greasy."

She wiped her hands on a towel,

as if readying them for the gift as he started to break the wrapper. Imitation gems in a pair of neat little clips glistened under the light when he had the tissue unfolded. Staring at them, Della's smile started to run out like the tide, but she allowed a segment to linger. Just enough to give a needling edge to her speech of acceptance.

"Thanks. They'll go nice with my Russian sables." Disregarding the clips she turned back to the canned stew.

Walt bit his under lip. He'd been doing a lot of lip biting lately. It was becoming more and more difficult to talk to her, to do things for her, to understand her. All right, he wasn't exactly setting the world on fire, but they weren't starving, either. They owned a house, the Mercury people were expanding his territory, and right now there was enough money in the bank account to afford a — Well, why talk about that again. There are some things you just can't rush.

They did talk about it again, late that night. They'd gone to a drive-in where a Bogart picture was playing. She liked Bogart. Della always said there was one guy who knew what made a woman tick. She could see it in his eyes. When a guy had that, he could make a woman crawl. Later they stopped off at a bar and killed a few beers. That earlier tension was gone. Della was even good for a couple of spicy stories.

Walking back from the garage, Walt's arm was around her waist. When they were in bed he slipped his arm under her neck. He never knew for sure with Della, but she hadn't cracked once about being tired, and he was more acutely aware of her perfumed scent, as though it might have been refreshed since their return.

He lay that way for a while watching a stealthy moonbeam on his ceiling. Then he turned, saying softly, "Honey, you know how much your being happy means to me."

Her own head stirred slightly. "Sure, Walt."

"Well, that savings account I opened last year . . . I've got it up to almost a grand —"

Her lips waltzed across his cheek. "Yes, dear?"

"Well, what I'm trying to say . . . now that we can afford it, don't you think we'd both be lots happier if we had a baby —"

He felt her sudden tensing. Her lips backed off, and her words were no longer whispered. "You're certainly the original bucket-boy, aren't you?"

"What do you mean?"

"You sure know when to rush out with the cold water."

"I'm sorry, Della. I just thought —"

"Yeah. You just thought I was going to be a brood mare like all the other ninnies in this crummy tract." She turned her back abruptly, curling the covers about her. "Well, you've got another guess coming, lover boy. I can think of a few other things I expect to get first out of our marriage."

Walt's stare was still on the ceiling long after the moonbeam had crept away. By morning resentment had been replaced by worry. Maybe Della had cause for those recent moods of hers. Can get pretty lonely for a housewife out here in the San Fernando Valley. Poor transportation. His using the car all day, and those business trips which kept him on the road part of each month. God knows he hadn't been providing her with much excitement lately. Even a married girl likes to get out once in a while. And when they looked like Della —

That's how Maury Fain happened to come out to the house the next night for dinner. Walt phoned her first in the afternoon.

"He just came up from El Centro, honey. One of my best accounts."

"Look. I know those hick merchants. When they come up to L.A., they want to step out. Make the town. You'll lose yourself an account, Pidgie, bringing him out to this place."

"No, not Maury. He's regular. You'll like him. Besides, being a bachelor he'll enjoy a home-cooked dinner for a change."

"That's a laugh. All we got in the house is hamburger. If I had my own car . . . which I *don't* . . . maybe I wouldn't mind shopping again today. But —"

"Don't worry, I'll bring home some big T-bones. Oh . . . there's another reason why I want to bring Maury out."

She said dully, "Okay, let's have the clincher."

"The boss gave me a pair of ringside seats for the fights at the Hollywood Legion tonight. Told me to take Maury. There's supposed to be a great card —"

"That's funny. I thought you were the boy who hated prizefights."

"That's the point, Della. I want you to go with him instead."

"*Me?* You getting broadminded, all of a sudden?"

"Oh . . . been thinking about things lately. Guess you don't get around as much as you should, Della. Thought you might enjoy the Legion fights tonight. All the stars usually go, and you'll be sitting right up front with them."

"Hmmmm. Okay, Pidgie, you've sold me a bill of goods. I could use an evening out. Bring him home."

When he introduced the man, Walt caught the glint of pleasant surprise in Della's eyes. Obviously Maury Fain was considerably removed from her concept of a border-town merchant. He was probably forty, but didn't look it, despite the dusting of gray in his hair. He had a good slender build, and the quietly self-assured look in his dark eyes of a man who had never been bothered with a woman shortage.

Dinner conversation was animated, with Della more like her old self. Walt made a mental note to invite more company to the house.

When she poured the second round of coffee, he decided it was time for his move. He pressed his temples, grimacing with a show of pain.

Della asked, going along with the act, "What's the matter, dear?"

"Oh, one of those headaches again. Can't seem to shake them lately." He turned to his guest. "Say, Maury, I'll only be a wet blanket tonight. Suppose Della goes with you instead. Mind terribly?"

Fain beamed roguishly. "*Mind?* Listen, I hope you have a headache every time I come up to L.A."

That was good for a general laugh.

When they drove off in his coupe, Walt read for a few hours, then went to bed. When he awakened, the illumined clock showed a quarter past three. His hand reached out and felt the cool unoccupied half of the bed. For about ten seconds there was a numbing feeling of anxiety and loneliness that evaporated at the sound of the back door being carefully closed. Della tiptoed into the room and started disrobing, without flicking on the light switch.

"Hello, Della."

"Oh. You still up?"

"Not long. Sure glad you're back. I started to worry when I saw the time."

"You don't ever have to worry about little Della. Would have been home long ago, but Maury insisted I stop off at the bar when I drove him back to the Ambassador."

"Have fun?"

"I guess you could call it that."

"That Maury, he's really got something, hasn't he?"

She slipped under the covers. "Yeah. He really has."

There was a marked pick-up in her attitude for the next week, or so, then it slid back into the old pattern. The day before he was to start on his Arizona trip, Della said, "I want to go with you this time."

"You kidding? Why, you'd die down there at this time of year."

"Can't be much worse than hanging around here alone."

"But, honey, you just couldn't take that weather. Look what a little heat up here does to you. Let's wait until —"

"Some *special* reason why you prefer to be alone on this trip?" There was a nasty inflection.

"You know there isn't any, Della. I've asked you to join me on others, but you never wanted to. Why insist on this one?"

"Because I'm getting bored silly. Can't you get that through your head?" Walt's look brought a softening shift in her tone. "Oh, come on, Pidgie, I've never visited any of those Mexican border towns. Maybe we could spend an evening at Nogales. Probably do us both good." She ran fingertips delicately along the edge of his ear. "See what I mean, baby?"

"Well, maybe if you just remember to stay out of the sun —"

They got away the next morning, long before dawn. Walt drove straight through to Calexico to spare her the discomfort of making the other stop-offs en route during the rising temperature.

It was still moderately comfortable when they checked into the big hotel. From their second-floor room she could see the busy port of entry at the international border. Anticipation glistened in her eyes. "Pidgie, I feel better already. Honest, you don't know how I needed this change."

He sorted the bags. "Good. You take it easy around the hotel today, while I backtrack to Brawley and those other towns. If you use the pool don't expose yourself to the sun too long."

"Don't worry about me. Maybe I'll cross over for a quick look at Mexicali while you're gone."

"Better not, Della. You'll start baking in another hour. Besides, you better get some sleep. We'll be driving through the night to Tucson, you know."

"I'm still going to see what it's like over there."

"Please, Della. Not during —" "He snapped his fingers suddenly. "Say, I got it. You rest up, and when I see Maury Fain over at El Centro, I'll ask him to join us for dinner over the line. That boy really knows the spots. How does that strike you?"

"Sounds all right."

"Sure you don't mind his coming along?"

"I'm your guest this trip, Pidgie. You make the plans."

She was still at the window. He kissed the back of her neck, saying softly, "Sorta hate to admit it, honey, but I'm real glad now you came along."

The nice feeling he'd enjoyed all morning sagged somewhat when he visited Fain's huge drugstore in El Centro later.

"Boss is up at Vegas," the cashier explained. "Won't be back for a couple of days."

Walt's let-down wasn't over any loss of business. Della loved to rhumba and they had some sizzling bands over in Mexicali. With a dancer like Maury along, she could have had herself a time tonight.

Although the sun had called it a day and was banking its fires along the rim of the Sierra Madres, the mercury still nudged one-twenty when he got back to the hotel. Opening his door, Walt's hand froze momentarily on the knob. Della was lying on the bed, a sheet outlining her nude body, and a wet towel across her forehead. There was a bowl of ice on the nightstand, and a bottle of aspirin. One hand drooped over the side of the bed.

"Honey, what's happened to you?"

There was an anguished sigh, then her eyes dragged open. "You were right, Walt. I should have listened to you. This heat's got me."

"What in the world did you do?"

"Oh, I went over to Mexicali. You know . . . all those cute little shops."

"I better call the house doctor. Sometimes heat exhaustion can be dangerous."

She shook her head. "No, I'll be all right by tomorrow. All I need is a good night's sleep."

"Guess that is the best remedy." A thought occurred to him, and he flopped concernedly into a chair. "Gee, I'd planned on our taking off for Tucson later tonight, so's to avoid the heat. Have to be there tomorrow if I want to nail that Maxwell account. Of course, if we have to stay over —"

"I got it, Pidgie. No sense losing that business over in Tucson. God knows we need it. You take off tonight, and I'll catch a plane tomorrow and meet you there. I'll be okay by then."

"No, honey, I couldn't leave you alone this way."

"Walt, you do like I say. Believe me, I'll be my old sweet self by tomorrow."

"Well —"

He left shortly after they had dinner in the room. Della didn't mind, at all. In fact, she insisted. This way he could catch Dave Harvey at his big store in Yuma. Dave never closed the place before eleven. Took only one hour to make the run.

It wasn't until he started giving Dave the build-up on the new Roxanne line of cosmetics, that he realized he'd left the sample kit back at the hotel. His easygoing client gave him a trial order, but he knew he'd never get away with it with old Ben Maxwell, over at Tucson. Ben had to feel, taste and smell before he ordered anything new, and introducing the Roxanne line was one of the main purposes of this trip.There was only one thing to do.

It wasn't quite midnight when he pulled into the parking area in front of the hotel, then went inside, silently rehearsing the cute little gag-line he'd thought up to explain his unscheduled return.

For the second time today, Walt stopped short upon entering their room. The shaded lamp on the nightstand splashed a yellow glow across the unoccupied bed. Walt glanced quickly into the bathroom. It was empty. Some damp towels were heaped under the lavatory. Della's nightgown was draped over the side of the tub. In that first surge of anxiety he thought she had become ill, going downstairs in search of the house physician. Then he became acutely aware of her large week-end case which hadn't been opened when he left. It was open now, and the new summer outfit she had brought along for evening wear was missing. There were other indications that hardly suggested a hasty departure in search of a doctor. The open manicure kit on the dresser, the imprint on a tissue of recently applied lipstick, a lingering scent of perfume. Walt fingered his jaw reflectively, then understanding began to seep through to him. You could hardly blame the girl. Cooped up in a lonely hotel room like this. She was probably down in the bar, right now, breaking the monotony over a cocktail. He felt better as he went down to the big lobby. He was rather glad it had turned out this way. Now they could have a drink together before he hit the road again. Latin music drifted from behind an obscure glass door. He pushed it open. A dark-haired singer was accompanying herself on a guitar. Most of the customers had swung around, watching the singer. Despite the dim-lighting, Walt didn't have to move in to realize his wife wasn't among the patrons.

The worries began to climb aboard again as he turned slowly and went back to the lobby. Of course, Della might have decided to visit one of those bistros in town. She knew how to handle herself, and there probably wasn't any particular danger, but the thought bothered him. Then it occurred to Walt to check with the room clerk. Why, sure. Why hadn't he done that in the first place? He went briskly to the desk.

The man looked over his shoulder at the key rack, then back at Walt. "No, sir. There's no message in the box, and I don't recall seeing her since I came on at eleven. Sorry."

Concern began to fan out on a large scale. A border town like Calexico was no place for a girl with Della's attractions to go slumming at this hour. He started for the street door. The only thing to do was check each bar until he located her.

He wasn't aware of the bellhop until he felt the light pressure on his arm. "Excuse me, sir. I think I see your wife tonight."

"Oh?" They were standing in the doorway now. He recognized the natty little Mexican who had brought in their luggage earlier. "Where was that?"

There was a subtle hesitation which Walt recognized. He hauled out a dollar. The man grinned his appreciation. "Thank you, sir. I see her about an hour ago. Just before I come to work. She was standing in front of the Caliente Club."

"Good. I'll go right over."

"I do not think you will find her there, sir."

"What makes you say that?"

"She met a man, and they drive away in his car."

Walt swallowed hard. "You sure?"

"Yes, sir. I know the fellow. Mr. Maury Fain."

"*Fain?* That's impossible. He's away on a trip."

"Oh, no, sir. I know Mr. Fain. He come here often. Lives in El Centro."

Walt moved to his car, and sat abstractedly at the wheel. He tried to hold on to one of the myriad thoughts splashing in his head. It had a comforting sound. At least, he knew Maury. There was really nothing to worry about now —.

Then the thought fragments fused,

and the searing flash of truth almost blinded him. God, how the pieces fitted now. Her late homecoming that first night with Fain. Her insistence on coming along on this trip, despite her loathing of intense heat. That fake exhaustion today, knowing he'd have to go on to Tucson without her. Even that touch about Fain being out of town. They'd certainly staged it beautifully. He started up the engine, backed sharply away from the parking area. He didn't think there would be much trouble now in locating Della. It was only six miles to El Centro.

He knew the house. Fain had brought him out for a visit on a previous trip. It was a one-acre layout, outside of town. Walt parked just beyond the place, then returned and vaulted the low fence. There was no moon but in the warm southwest night he had no trouble in reconnoitering the darkened home. He stuck to the grass. Muted radio music drifted from an open window in the rear. He moved alongside, waiting against the wall. Occasionally there were subdued voices. Finally he heard the man say, "Think he'd beat you up, if he found out?"

She laughed. A throaty laugh. "Him? Why he can't stand to harm a bug. Honest, not even a bug."

"I'd beat you up, if you tried it on me, baby."

She purred, "With you, maybe I wouldn't mind —" The rest was lost in a smothered sigh.

Walls collapsed inside him. First, he fought sickness, then an impulse more compelling than any he had ever known. No, that wasn't the way. That wasn't the way, at all. He unclenched his hands, rubbing one across his moist forehead. Then he trudged back to his car. He found a dirt road and parked there for the rest of the night. Sleep didn't come until the first red feelers of dawn crept out into the sky.

He returned to the hotel around nine-thirty. As he anticipated she was back in the bed. She blinked drowsily through her surprise. "Well . . . how come you're back so soon?"

"Had some engine trouble in Yuma."

"Oh." She added, very casually, "Where did you sleep last night?"

"In Yuma. How are you feeling, Della?"

"I'm okay."

"Guess that rest fixed you up."

"Yeah. That's what I needed."

"Well, good. You get dressed and we'll leave for Tucson."

The car bounced as it slipped out of the caked rut. Walt had driven eight miles along this desert trail since leaving the paved highway. It was one of those unmapped roads that seem to lose themselves in the endless mesquite and sand. The sand that dusted this one indicated it had been long unused.

Della awoke, then stiffened. "How in hell did you get here?"

"It's a short cut. Saves us about twenty miles to Gila Bend."

"Yeah? And what happens if we get stuck? Just wait around for the vultures?"

"Don't worry, Della. I know these roads."

For a while she sulked silently in her corner. Above them, the sun stalked their car, like a vengeful flame-thrower. Rivulets were coursing down her pale skin. By the time the speedometer clicked off another mile, breathing had become an effort.

She finally rasped, "I can't stand any more of this! Turn around and go back to the highway. You hear?"

"Whatever you say, Della."

"I say it!"

He braked, looked out on his side, then shook his head.

"Mighty narrow here. You better step out and direct me while I back around."

"*Me?* Nothing doing. I don't want to broil to death."

"You're a cinch to, if we ever get stuck in that sand on the side."

"Well . . . okay."

When she was outside, Walt rolled down his window, maneuvering the Chevy with extreme care. Coming out of the final turn, he pulled ahead three lengths before she shouted.

"Hey! I'm not in the car yet, you fool!"

The coupe continued moving.

"Walt, stop that car! You out of your mind?" She had started to run after it. The gap never quite closed. Her cry was a fearful entreaty now. "Walter, what are you doing to me? What are you doing —"

He put his head out of the window. "Just keeping my promise, Della."

"Prom —? I don't understand."

"Never to lay a finger on you in anger . . . no matter what you did. Remember now?"

"Yes, yes. But this doesn't make sense."

"I think it does, Della. You see, I didn't really stop over in Yuma last night."

Her eyes became panicky discs in that one terrible instant of comprehension. "No, darling . . . please . . . please —"

Walt shifted into high.

"Please . . . Oh, dear God . . . please —"

Through the rear vision mirror he could see her receding figure, arms outstretched. Three times she stumbled. The last time she remained face down in the sand.

Walt bit his lip until there was pain. Then he fed the car more gas.

Response

"Every man has his price," Stone said. "You're no exception. All I have to do is find it . . ."

BY

ARNOLD MARMOR

JOSE ABRARDO entered his small, inexpensively furnished study and smiled at the young man who had asked to see him.

"I trust I haven't kept you waiting long," Abrardo said.

The young man got to his feet and took off his hat. "Not at all," he said. He grinned at Abrardo, a boyish grin, his white teeth almost translucent against his tanned face. "My name's Ned Stone."

Abrardo nodded. "I know. I was warned about you before you set foot on the island, Mr. Stone. The Miami police sent my chief of police a wire." He was nearing sixty, with a fat body that sweated almost continuously. His head was completely bald, and his flesh-embedded eyes twinkled in appreciation of the game he knew would follow. "I know your reputation, Mr. Stone," he went on, "and I believe I know what you want." He motioned to a chair. "Please be seated."

"Thank you," Stone said, and sat down. "I'll come right to the point. I represent a group of business people who are interested in this island as a base for their operations."

Abrardo smiled politely. "And their business?"

"Gambling. In short, I'm here to bribe you."

Abrardo nodded, sighed, and sat down opposite Stone. The chair creaked under his weight. "I knew it," he said. "My friend, do you think you are the first to approach me?" He shook his head as if answering his own question. "No. There have been many others. But you see —" he shrugged his shoulders — "I am an honest man. So I must turn you down."

"I know something of human nature," Stone said. "Every man has his price. I don't give a damn who he is." He looked steadily at Abrardo. "What's yours?"

Abrardo shook his head. "Please. I've been an honest man all my life — both before and after I became a government official, Mr. Stone. I'm too old to change now."

Stone leaned forward. "What about five thousand dollars?" he asked. "Good American money."

Abrardo laughed. "You are joking."

"Ten thousand?"

"Would you like a drink?"

"Sure," Stone said.

"Pedro!" Abrardo called. "Make us some drinks."

"We can't operate without your okay," Stone said. "This is a big play. It involves gambling casinos, floating crap games — the works." He paused. "Have you ever been off this island?"

"No," Abrardo said. "This is my home. I have never had to leave."

"Haven't you ever thought about leaving? Seeing other places, other countries?"

"I am a lonely man," Abrardo said. "A lonely man has many thoughts."

"You could do with a pile of hard cash," Stone said.

Pedro came in with the drinks. He handed one to each of the men, nodded to Abrardo, and left.

Stone raised his glass. "To a better understanding," he said.

Abrardo smiled, and said nothing.

Stone put his glass down on a small table. "Will you think about it?" he asked.

"There is nothing to think about," Abrardo said.

"You told me there were others before me," Stone said. "Maybe they never reached your price."

"Must I have a price?" Abrardo asked.

"You're human, aren't you? I'll get to your price yet. You'll give in, all right. But it would save us time if I knew how much you want." He smiled. "I can go pretty high."

"No," Abrardo said. "That's my final answer."

"Okay, then — I'll double the ten thousand."

"Please, Mr. Stone. I have many things to do." Abrardo stood up and glanced toward the door.

"Can I see you again?" Stone asked.

"Of course. My home is always open to you."

Stone got to his feet. "I'll wire

my boss," he said. "Tomorrow I might have an offer you couldn't possibly turn down."

"You seem very sure of yourself, my friend," Abrardo said.

"I haven't failed yet."

"You may be in for a surprise."

"I don't think so," Stone said. He put on his hat. "I'll see you tomorrow."

Abrardo watched him go. A lonely man has many thoughts, he reflected. He had never been even close to being rich in his sixty years. The years had given him much fat and nothing more. He thought of the things he could do with money. There were so many things to see, so many countries to visit. He could do all the things he had always dreamed of doing.

But the price?

He could never again think of himself as an honest man. There would be no more integrity. . . . He walked to the window and watched Stone driving up the road. What a beautiful car, he thought. So long and black and shiny. . . .

Suddenly he realized he was sweating.

The next morning was clear and bright, and the yellow rays of the early sun made the island glisten like burnished copper.

Jose Abrardo stood at the window of his study as Stone's car drew up in front of the house. He saw the look of confidence on Stone's face as he jumped from the car and ran up to the door, and then he sighed and turned around to wait for him.

Stone's teeth flashed even more whitely than they had the day before. He crossed to Abrardo and extended a small blue envelope.

Abrardo shook his head. "Please, Mr. Stone. I told you —"

Stone laughed. "It isn't money. That part comes later. This is just a little token of good will, from the boss."

Abrardo took a letter knife from his desk and slit the envelope. In it were two credit cards, one with an international airline and the other with a world-wide hotel chain. He glanced up at Stone.

"Just a token," Stone said. "They're in your name, you'll notice, and they're good for a year. Go anywhere you like to go, and stay at the finest hotels. There's no limit, and those cards are good all over the world."

He's so sure of himself, Abrardo thought. So certain his money can buy anything. An automobile, a man — anything. He glanced about the room at the worn furniture that had already been old when he came into office so many years ago. In all those years he had never been able to buy one new thing for this room. There were so many other things, like the charities to which he contributed, that there had never been enough money even to replace the threadbare carpeting.

And he saw, suddenly, that what was true of the room was equally true of the rest of his life. And yet, the well-worn furniture and his cheap clothing were symbols of his honesty. However much he might have yearned for things, these symbols were here to remind him that he had something beyond the reach of money. Integrity. Integrity, and the knowledge that he had done a hard job well.

He took a deep breath, held it a moment, then let it out slowly and replaced the credit cards in the envelope. He handed the envelope back to Stone.

Stone brushed it aside. "Like I said, it's just a token. Just a little something from the boss." His smile grew wider. "I told you I might have an offer you couldn't possibly turn down. I was right. I could hardly believe it myself when I found out how high the boss would go."

"Please, Mr. Stone," Abrardo said. "We have been through all this before. I assure you my answer will always be no, and —"

"You'll change your mind, once you hear our offer."

Abrardo shrugged wearily and gestured toward the papers on his desk. "I have much to do today . . ."

Stone stepped close, still smiling, and softly named the amount.

A little later, Abrardo stood quite still in the middle of the small room, staring down at the lifeless body of Ned Stone. There was a dark, widening stain on the front of Stone's shirt, and from the exact middle of the stain protruded the haft of Abrardo's paper knife.

A full minute went by, and then Abrardo called out sharply to Pedro.

He heard Pedro running toward the study. The servant stopped in the doorway, his eyes wide, looking first at Stone and then at Abrardo. Abrardo sighed. "It seems we were both right, Pedro," he said. "I am too honest. All my life I have been honest. It would have been worse than death for me to change."

"But . . . what happened?" Pedro asked.

Abrardo looked down at the dead man. "He finally reached my price."

CRIME CAVALCADE

BY VINCENT H. GADDIS

Dreaming True

George Stavrakas, owner of a Washington, D. C., restaurant, woke up in a cold sweat one night after dreaming his place was being robbed. The dream was so vivid that he quickly dressed and ran to his restaurant a block away. His dream was true — he could see three burglars ransacking the place. A few moments later the police had the trio in custody.

Hide and Seek

In Toledo, Ohio, John P. Rosentreter has had the life-long habit of looking under the bed each night before retiring. One recent Monday night he went through the usual routine, and blinked his eyes. Grabbing his rifle he called police. Officers arrived and arrested a prowler for burglary.

Hunger Trap

Daniel Duran, a young Mexican, sneaked over the U. S. border at Tia Juana. After traveling for 15 days, mostly at night to avoid detection, he began to get pretty hungry. He saw a farm, climbed over a barbed wire fence, and asked for a job. He got it! It was the Los Angeles county sheriff's honor farm.

Art Critic

Police in Hamilton, Ont., were puzzled as they searched for the thieves who stole a 250-pound cornerstone for a new art gallery building. All the stone contained was several coins, postage stamps, newspapers and a list of contributors. Officers theorized that, "It must have been someone who didn't like modern art."

Fate Fantasy

It happened in Philadelphia several months ago. A young woman who had been waiting for her boy friend for over an hour at a street corner, finally decided he had stood her up. As she turned to go home, she saw his car pass by, but her friend was not driving.

She ran to Patrolman Russell Stein, standing nearby, and told him her suspicions. The officer took off in pursuit and succeeded in stopping the car and arresting the 15-year-old driver. The woman then accompanied them to the police station, where she found her boy friend reporting the theft of his automobile.

TV Triumphs

Mr. and Mrs. A. C. Saylors said they were so engrossed in a television program in their Sacramento,

Calif. home, that they did not notice it when an unidentified assailant fired seven shots into their living room, shattering a mirror on the wall.

And in Elkhart, Ind., a window peeper apprehended after numerous complaints told police he was merely watching television. "Couldn't afford to buy a set of my own," he added.

Embezzlement Enigma

Several years ago Henry Chancey, a Boston, Mass., railway mail clerk, reported the disappearance of $30,000 of Federal Reserve cash in transit. After an intensive investigation, federal agents decided that Chancey had taken the money himself. However, the suspected man had a good reputation and no definite evidence could be turned up against him.

But inquiries revealed that Chancey was a sleepwalker. As a last resort detectives decided to try questioning him while he was asleep. To their astonishment, Chancey not only answered all their questions fully but, still in deep slumber, led them several miles from his home to an abandoned well, where they found the missing money intact.

Baffled Burglars

After burglars made off with his 600-pound safe in St. Louis, Mo., Ernest J. Hilgert, a gasoline company operator, had a running battle by telephone with the thieves. A few hours after the robbery a stranger called Hilgert at his home and said, "Well, Ernie, we finally got your safe." Hilgert explained that two previous attempts had been made to steal the safe. On the following day the same man called again and asked Hilgert for the combination, adding that he and his companions had been unsuccessful in their efforts to get to the $265 in cash. Hilgert refused to oblige. The thief made three more calls on successive days pleading for the combination before he finally gave up. Hilgert lost no time installing a new, 1200-pound vault.

Bargain Day

Shoppers in Newark, N. J., rubbed their eyes in astonishment at a sign on a store reading: "Smuggled Diamonds for Sale." However, the offer was legal. The store had purchased the stones from the government, which had confiscated them as contraband.

Where's the Money?

There had to be a way out — if Joe could only find it. But Joe was blind . . .

BY

FLOYD MAHANNAH

THEY worked it so fast, and so neat, that at first I didn't realize what was happening.

I was driving home from work; it was after dark, and I was passing through a new section of unfinished homes and vacant lots. This big car had pulled alongside me and a little ahead; then suddenly it cut in, crowding me so I had to hit the brake hard. The other guy hit his brake too, kept riding it, and kept crowding me over until we both came to a stop with me pinched against the curb.

My first thought was cops. But cops would have used the siren.

Then both doors of the big car popped open, and two guys came out moving fast; and suddenly I knew what was happening. I gunned the motor, trying to make my Ford jump the curb, but it was too high. All I did was stall the motor. And there was no time to start it again.

I hit the door handle, and came out running.

In the dark, cutting around the unfinished houses and across vacant lots the way I was, I might have outrun them if I hadn't tripped over something in the waist-high grass. For seconds I was flat on my face, seeing stars; then I rolled over, and these two black shapes were coming at me, one of them letting go a hoarse, bubbly laugh as they piled into me.

Nobody ever laughed like that but Dutch Labeau.

In the dark, it was a mess. It was fists and elbows and knees, more misses than hits; but I wasn't doing too badly, because they were hitting each other as often as me. I don't know which one pulled the gun — nor why, because they sure didn't want me dead — not until I'd told them where the money was, anyway. But a gun did go off, squarely in my face, it seemed like; and after that I was half stunned, and I couldn't see a thing. All I remember is a confusion of slugging and gouging in the blackness, and me letting go a yell whenever I got breath, hoping to bring help from some place. The next thing I knew, a siren was wailing, and after that I was alone for a while in the blackest night I ever saw. Then footsteps, and a voice out of the blackness:

"You all right, mister?"

"I — I don't know —"

"Jesus," another voice said, "look at his eyes."

I sat in the hospital while the doctor finished his examination, and it was still like there was no light left in the world. I couldn't see a thing. All I had was the quiet sound of heels on linoleum, the sharp hospital smell in my nose, and pain like a knife in my head. The doctor didn't say anything, just bandaged my eyes; and when he was done, I said:

"Will I be — blind?"

"It's too early to tell."

"How soon can you tell?"

"A week. Maybe two."

"I want to phone my wife."

Then from somewhere out of the black emptiness, rank cigar smoke drifted, and the heavy cop voice of Detective Lieutenant Herendeen said:

"What did you do with the hundred and twenty thousand dollars, Joe?"

"Nothing. I never had it."

"Don't kid me. Where's that money?"

In the last twelve years I must have answered that question a million times. And always the same way:

"I don't know."

"Dutch Labeau thinks you do."

"Dutch is crazy. Have you picked him up yet?"

"On what grounds would we pick

him up? A laugh you heard in the dark? How long do you think we could hold him on a thing like that?"

It wasn't a matter of grounds. If he wanted to pick up Dutch, he would. He didn't want to. And I knew why. He was saying:

"I admit it figures. You cut Dutch and Lennie out of their share on that bank job. Now they're out of prison, and they want their dough. Where is it, Joe?"

A million and one times.

"I don't know. Look, if I'd had it, I could have turned it in, gone state's evidence, and gotten off with a year. I was young, it was my first offense, and the D.A. offered me that deal. You think I'd have served six stinking years in the pen, if I didn't have to?"

"For twenty thousand bucks a year? I think you would."

"God Almighty, Herendeen, that job was twelve years ago. I did the time, and I've gone straight. I'm a foreman in an iron foundry, I'm married, I have a three-year-old daughter, I owe nine thousand bucks on my home, and six hundred on my car. Does any of that sound like a guy with a hundred and twenty G's in his pocket?"

"Dutch Labeau kidnapping you sounds like it."

"Dutch is half nuts, and you know it. He's got it in that twisted head of his that I made off with all the dough. He's had twelve years to chew on the goofy idea; and he's sworn to get either me or the dough. And he's just as liable as not to grab my wife or my kid to put the squeeze on me. Where's that phone?"

There was a moment of silence. The doctor whispered something impatiently to him; then Herendeen's slow, harsh voice came back at me from the dark:

"I'll make you a deal. Turn in the dough, and I'll see nobody touches you or your wife or your kid. I'll leave you in the clear too — I'll say it was an anonymous tip. After all, you served your time for it."

Which was the reason he hadn't picked up Dutch and Lennie. They were his lever to put the pressure on me. God, wasn't there any way to convince him I didn't know where the money was? It was hard to think straight, the way my head hurt; and in the end, all I said was:

"I want to phone my wife."

"Where's that money?"

The million and second time.

To hell with it. I stood up, and I started walking toward where I figured the door was. I hit something — a table or a chair — I went sideways into something else that turned over with sound like a whole china cabinet hitting the floor; then I tripped and fell into the middle of it, and the way that doctor was cussing would curl your hair.

But I got action.

I got a phone, and a nurse dialled it, and Peg's worried voice answered.

"Hello?"

"It's me, Peg."

"About time." A smile in her voice for me. "Where have you been?"

"Something happened, Peg."

"Something bad?" She'd gotten it from the sound of my voice. I could almost see her face turning serious — see the shining brown hair, gray eyes, firm chin, and the perky dress she'd have put on so she'd look nice for me. I said:

"Is Corinne there?"

"Of course. That is, she's next door, playing with the Perkins children."

The Perkins had lights in their side yard, and sometimes the kids played out there after dark. I said:

"Go see if she's there. Bring her home."

"What's wrong, Joe?"

"Do what I said. I'll hold on."

"Well — all right."

I held on, and in the next room I could hear the doctor still cussing; and in this room I could smell Herendeen's cigar, but Herendeen didn't say a word. Then Peg's voice:

"She isn't there."

"You're sure?"

"Little Buddy Perkins says somebody picked her up in a car. He thought it was you." There was a tremor in her voice, and I knew she was getting scared. "Was it?"

I was scared myself now. I was as scared as a man can get, but I kept my voice steady: "No."

"Joe, where is she?"

I was scared, but I knew what I had to do. Keep it from Herendeen. Dutch was crazy, and if the law crowded him, he'd be liable to panic — kill Corinne, put the body where it'd never be found, and run for it. There was only one way I could be sure of getting Corinne back safely.

"Everything's fine —" I forced my voice to be normal — "and I'll be home in a little while."

"*But where is Corinne?*"

"I'll be home in a few minutes. Tell you all about it."

"*Joe* —"

I hung up. My voice had been steady, my hands weren't shaking, I was doing all the right things; but thinking about Corinne in Dutch's hands was like dying as each second ticked by. But I mustn't hurry. Herendeen's voice came out of the blackness:

"The kid okay?"

"Sure."

"I'll have one of my boys run you home."

"To hell with you and your whole department."

He didn't say anything. I could hear him turn and walk out; then I had the nurse call a taxi for me.

Peg screamed softly when she saw my bandaged eyes. I said: "It's all right. Pay the cab driver, will you?"

She paid him, and he left. We went inside, and I could feel her shaking hand on my arm.

"What happened to your eyes?"

She already had enough to be scared about. I told her, "It's nothing. The doctor says they'll be as good as new in a couple of days. Now about Corinne —"

I told her everything that had happened, and where Corinne was, and Peg spun away from me.

"*We've got to call the police!*"

"*No!*" I grabbed for her, and missed. Then she was dialling the phone, and I located her by the sound of it, fumbled for the phone, got it away from her and back onto the hook; and Peg had started to cry.

"*She's been kidnapped, and* —"

"And if we put the cops on Dutch, he'll do something crazy. The rap for kidnapping would be the same as for murder, and he knows it. Put the law on him, and he might kill Corinne, hide her body, and run."

"But what *can* we do?"

"Sit tight. He'll contact us."

"It's — it's the hundred and twenty thousand he wants, isn't it?"

"Yes."

"But you can't give it to him. You haven't got it."

"He thinks I have."

"What are you going to do?"

"Get Corinne back."

"How?"

The phone was ringing. I held out my hand. "Let me." Peg handed it to me, and I said, "Hello?"

"Joe?"

"Yes."

He laughed then, that crazy laugh of his that was like a lot of bubbles in his throat. And the laugh brought up the picture of him: the gaunt face with its broken nose, thick crooked lips, eyes like black glass. He said:

"Want your kid back?"

"Yes. Is she all right?"

"Sure. For now. You ain't done nothing stupid like calling the cops?"

"No."

"I want that dough, Joe."

"I've got it."

"I want it, and I ain't fooling."

"Not a cent until I get Corinne back."

"Listen, stupid, I'm in the driver's seat. Not you." His voice sounded like he'd turned away from the phone. "Come here, kid. I got your old man on the phone."

I gripped the phone hard, then Corinne's clear, childish voice came over it:

"Daddy?"

"Sure, honey. Where are you?"

"I don't know. Daddy, I want to go home."

"Sure. In a little while."

"I'm hungry."

"Supper's all ready. It'll only be a little while."

Dutch laughed, Corinne whimpered, then screamed: "*Daddy!*"

"Dutch!" I yelled. "*Dutch!*"

"I only twisted her arm a little."

"If you harm her —" my voice was shaking — "I'll kill you, Dutch. *I'll kill you!*"

"What's all this talk about killing? I'm talking about money."

"We'll talk money when my kid's safe. Not before."

"Listen, stupid —"

"You listen. I'll meet you any place you say. When you've got me, you can release her. And when I'm satisfied she's safe, I'll talk."

He was silent. He would be picking it apart in his mind, his black eyes hooded and wary, trying to find a trap someplace in it. Finally he said:

"Okay. Get in your car and drive to —"

"Dutch, I'm blind."

"What?"

"The flash and burn from that gun going off."

He laughed suddenly like it was a big joke. "Well, I'll be damned. Blind."

"I can take a taxi. I'll wait alone for you on any corner or any place you say."

More silence while he picked that one apart. Then: "All right. The northeast corner of Eleventh and Rivercrest. And no tricks —" his voice turned soft and deadly — "or you'll never see this brat again."

"I'll be waiting. And —" He'd hung up on me. I gave Peg the phone, and told her:

"He agreed to release Corinne. He didn't say where, but it'll probably be close enough for her to walk home. As soon as she's safe, call the police — Herendeen is the one to ask for. He'll pull in the F.B.I."

"You have no money to give him, Joe. What will he do to you?"

"We won't worry about that until Corinne's safe. You call the cops then, and I'll stall him any way I can."

Her arms were around me hard now, and she was starting to cry again. I said:

"No time for that, kid. Phone for a taxi."

Peg rode down with me in the taxi, helped me out, and steered me across to the northeast corner.

"Joe, I'm — I'm scared. Maybe we should call the police first —"

"Corinne comes first. You go home. And if she isn't there in an hour, go ahead and call the cops."

She clung to me, and she wasn't crying now, just shivering like she was cold. Then I felt her cold lips on mine, and her whisper:

"I'll — be seeing you, Joe."

"Sure."

Then she was gone, and the sound of the cab died away in the dark.

A man newly blind is the loneliest man in the world. It's like they took the whole universe away and left you hanging alone in the endless blackness.

I tried to light a cigarette, but I burned my fingers, and got the cigarette lit all crooked so it wouldn't draw right. I threw it away, and put the lighter back in my pocket. It was a sterling silver lighter with "To Joe with love from Peg" engraved on it. That had been last Christmas when Peg and Corinne —

I don't know how long I thought about it, but I know I didn't come up with a thing. Then brakes squealed softly, a car door opened, and a voice said:

"All right, Joe. Into the back seat."

That was the voice of Chick — I remembered it from twelve years ago. Big, dumb Chick who thought Dutch Labeau was the biggest shot of them all. They made a pair, all right.

I stumbled getting into the car, and I could feel Chick's clumsy hands frisking me.

"He's clean, Dutch."

Then the hat was lifted from my head, the dark glasses snatched away, then came Dutch's bubbly laugh:

"Blind as a bat! Ain't that something?"

Chick laughed because Dutch did, then he let out the clutch and the car started moving. Dutch said:

"Where's the dough, Joe?"

"When I talk to my wife on the phone, and she tells me my kid is home and unharmed, I'll tell you where the money is."

"You know I keep my word."

"I know you're a lying rat."

The bubbly laugh, like I'd paid him a compliment. Then: "I'll send the kid home. After that, sweetheart —" his voice turned cold with twelve years of bottled up hate — "we'll see about you."

I drew a long breath then. Corinne was going to be safe. I thought about that, and for a second I felt good. Then I thought about me, and I didn't feel good at all.

I was sitting in a dusty-smelling room we'd climbed a flight of stairs to get to. Chick had gone someplace in the car — to take Corinne home, Dutch said. She hadn't been in the place when we got there — at least I hadn't heard her — and when I asked Dutch where she was, he just gave me that laugh of his, and went on trying to pump me about the money. I sat silent, sweating, and more than a little sick.

Then steps came up the stairs, the door opened, and Chick said: "Okay. She's home."

I said, "I want to hear my wife say it."

"Sure." Dutch dialled a phone, waited, said, "Here," and a phone was put in my hand. I said:

"Peg?"

"Yes. Are you all right, Joe?"

"Is Corinne home?"

"Yes. I called the police. Where are you?"

"I —"

That was all. Dutch had broken the connection. He said:

"Okay, that's the deal. Now where's the dough?"

That was the deal, all right. Corinne was safe, the cops and the G-men were on the job, and me — where was I? I was sitting in the blackest night in the world, with a crazy killer who I was pretty sure meant to kill me whether he got the money or not. As I said, he had nothing to lose — the penalty for kidnapping would be the same as for murder — and he hated me enough and was crazy enough to kill me.

"*Where's that hundred and twenty grand, Joe?*"

"What makes you think I've even got that money, Dutch?"

"You said —"

"That was so you'd turn Corinne loose."

"Don't stall me, God damn it. When we came out of that bank, you were carrying the money. All of it. What did you do with it?"

"I jumped into the car with Sid, and that was about the time the police car got there, caught you and Chick at the door of the bank and drove you back inside. We got away, but Sid was wounded — hurt bad. We made it to the hideout, and I left Sid there with the money, while I went for a doctor he said we could trust. The cops grabbed me on the way."

"What are you trying to say?"

"That I left the dough with Sid."

"Don't snow me. When the cops got to the hideout, Sid was dead and the dough was gone."

"Maybe the cops got it."

"Like hell. You left Sid to die, you stashed the dough someplace, tried for a getaway and got caught. *Where's that dough?*"

The same question — how many times was that? I said, "I don't know."

I could hear him breathing hard, standing so close to me I could smell his rotten teeth. Then he hit me across the eyes, and pain exploded inside my skull. Dimly I realized the blow had knocked me and the chair over backwards; then I was on the floor, being kicked and being cussed, and finally the deeper blackness that was unconsciousness washed over me.

I don't know how long I was out. I came around with somebody throwing water in my face, and Dutch yelling:

"Where's that dough?"

That went on a while, and finally I sat up, sick every way there was.

"*God damn it, where's that dough?*"

I had to think . . . stall . . . think of something . . . I said, "All right — I'll tell you —"

"That's better."

It had to be something reasonable, something he'd believe, something it would take time to check:

"I — I buried it."

"Buried it where?"

"Near the river."

"Where near the river?"

"Back of the levee — a mile or so north of the old hideout."

"How'll we find it?"

"I'd have to show you."

"You'll tell me. *Now!*"

"I'd have to show you the landmarks."

Silence while he thought it over. Maybe he didn't believe it. Maybe they were getting ready to work me over again. Then Dutch's voice rasped:

"All right. On your feet. And this better not be a stall. It's a pleasure to work you over, baby. And it'll be a pleasure to kill you too, you doublecrossing son of a bitch!"

He hadn't meant to let that out — the part about killing me — but that's what he meant to do, and he'd meant to do it all along. As soon as he got the money, or as soon as he was sure he wasn't going to get it, I was going to die.

It's a hard thing, to know you're going to be dead in a little while. Knowing a thing like that ought to make a man's brain work twice as fast. Maybe it did, but I still couldn't see any way out of the nightmare. I couldn't see anything. Just blackness.

I knew what the river looked like along there.

The road ran along the top of the levee, and at this particular spot there was an old landing where they used to load grain onto the river boats in the old days. The nearest house was almost a quarter of a mile away. There was just the levee with the cottonwoods and willows growing on it, and the rotten piling of the old landing sticking out into the river. Only a week ago Peg and Corinne and I had been fishing from that landing.

Only a week? It seemed years ago, and in another world.

Dutch was saying, "There's your landing with a big cottonwood at one end, like you said."

"Is there an iron bollard at the other end of the landing?"

"An iron what?"

"A post, sort of."

"Wait'll I put the flash on it. Yeah, there it is."

"In the old days they used to tie the riverboats —"

"To hell with where they tied the boats. Where's that dough?"

We were standing beside the car, me with my back to it and leaning against it. I was trying to fix the picture in my mind: I would be facing the landing about ten feet from it, the landing itself would be about fifteen feet wide, and beyond that and ten feet below it would be the river. Could I run for it? Dive into the river? I was a good enough swimmer, and in the darkness maybe I could get away? Not a chance. They'd catch me in two steps; or, failing that, put a slug in my back before I'd gone four. If only there was some way to create a diversion, something to take their eyes off me — but how would I know when they were off?

"Come on, where's that dough?"

"Let me think. You take a line from that cottonwood to the iron bollard. And let's see — ten steps, was it? No, twenty —"

"Make up your mind." Dutch was getting suspicious.

I was hoping for a car to pass, but few would at night. And if I'd picked a more public place, Dutch would never believe I'd have buried money there. All I could do was stall:

"Twenty feet, it is. Twenty feet from the bollard. Now let's see —"

It was all borrowed time. A little

longer to breathe, to feel the cool drift of night air on my face, smell the cleanness of growing things —

"*Where's the dough?*"

I had my hand on the rear fender to steady myself. I could feel the little flap you opened to put gas in the tank; and I was thinking illogically that a blind man would have to learn to read with his fingers. And my brain, which had been racing for an hour without coming up with a thing, suddenly put two things together as quick as you'd snap your fingers.

And my hands had moved almost as quickly. One had snapped up the little flap behind my back, and was twisting the gas tank cap; and the other hand — the one in my pocket — was coming out with the cigarette lighter. The cap was off now, I whirled, my thumb snapping the cigarette lighter, shoving it at the open tank neck, as I pulled as far to one side as I could — snapping the cigarette lighter again and again because I didn't know if it had lighted or not.

Maybe it wasn't lighting, or maybe I wasn't holding it close enough — all I know is that the explosion never came. Dutch yelled:

"What the —"

Then the lighter was batted from my hand, a fist came out of the empty blackness, but it only glanced off my jaw. And suddenly I realized I had my diversion — and I had sense enough to spin away and start running for the river.

Somebody tackled me, but it was only halfway effective — I was down, but I was still rolling across the rotten boards of the landing. Somebody jumped on me, but I got my arms around him, and now the two of us were rolling. Then we were at the edge of the landing, one of my legs was in open air, and I put all my strength into a final shove.

We went over.

Falling, Dutch's wild yell blasted my ear, then the river cut it off, and we sank, still locked and struggling. I was as big a man as Dutch, and in the water I was as good a man, because his eyes couldn't help him now. And I had more wind. He'd wasted his on that yell, while I'd sucked in all I could on the way down.

I didn't fight him. I just held on, and that was fighting enough. It seemed like a hundred years I hung onto his wildly threshing body, while the fast current swept us along. At long last the threshing got weaker, finally died altogether; but I held on grimly until I knew that whether Dutch was faking it or not, I was going to die myself unless I got some air.

I turned him loose, and he hadn't been faking it. I swam for the surface, but Dutch stayed where he was.

I sucked in big gulps of air, and the taste of it was the sweet taste of life itself. We had drifted a long ways in that fast current, because somewhere out there in the darkness I could hear Chick's voice bawling, "Hey, Dutch, where are you? Answer me, Dutch," and it sounded a good sixty or seventy feet away.

I drifted, shucking my coat and shoes, and Chick's yells got farther and farther away, and I knew then I was safe.

I don't know how far I drifted. I didn't know which way to swim to reach shore, so I just drifted, and after a long time I could hear music — a radio, I guess — coming across the water. I swam that way, yelling for help, and it was only a few minutes more before I got it.

But that wasn't the end of it.

I had two long, black weeks in the hospital with nothing to do but think — you do a lot of thinking when you're blind — then they took off the bandages, and I could see a little, and the doctor said that eventually I'd be able to see as good as ever. Then he put the bandages back on.

He went away, and I was alone in the dark again, waiting. Then the door opened, and a rank smell of cigar smoke came into the room. I said:

"It took you a long time, Herendeen."

"What did you want to see me about?"

"The dough. It's buried in fruit jars in back of an abandoned barn on Mulberry Road."

I could hear him let out a long breath, then there was only the drifting smoke to say he was still there. Finally he said:

"Where, exactly?"

I told him where, exactly, and I could hear him writing it down. Then he said in an odd voice, not like a cop at all:

"After all these years — why are you turning it in?"

"I'm tired of it."

"Yet you risked your life holding out on Dutch."

"He meant to kill me anyway."

"You're just — tired of it?"

"Sick and tired. I've had twelve years of worrying about that money, and that's enough. Besides, I learned something while Dutch held Corinne prisoner — something about myself."

"And what was that?"

"My wife and kid mean more to me than any amount of dough. I guess that's why I've kept it buried all these years — if Peg knew I had it, she'd leave me."

I drew a long breath and finished it: "I've got a damned good life, Herendeen. And there's no room in it for stolen money."

Herendeen didn't speak for so long I thought he wasn't going to. Then his voice came from the door, and it was a dry, cop's voice again: "Well, I've got to go check an anonymous tip on some stolen money."

Anonymous — that took the last of the load off my mind. And, much later, when the nurse came in to ask how I felt, I told her the truth:

"I've never felt better in my life."

The Beat-Up Sister

A Lew Archer Novelette

BY

JOHN ROSS MACDONALD

Everybody agreed Dewar was the killer —even after Archer found Dewar's corpse.

I PICKED her up on the Daylight. We had adjacent chairs, and fell into conversation. Or maybe she picked me up. With some girls, the ones who play the game subtly, you never know.

She was very young, and when she leaned sideways to hear my deathless comments on the landscape and the weather, she wafted spring odors towards me. She had a flippant nose and wide blue eyes, the kind that men like to call innocent. Her blonde hair bubbled like boiling gold around her small blue hat. She laughed in the right places, a little hectically. But in between the laughter, there was a certain somberness in her eyes, a pinched look around her mouth. When I invited her to join me in the buffet car for a drink, she said:

"Oh no. Really. Thank you. I couldn't."

"Why not?"

"I'm not twenty-one, for one thing. You wouldn't want to contribute to the delinquency of a minor?"

"It sounds like pleasant work."

She veiled her eyes and looked away. The hills plunged backward past the train window like giant green dolphins against the flat blue background of the sea. The afternoon sun was bright on her hair. I hoped I hadn't offended her. She appealed to my paternal instincts. Call them paternal.

After a long minute she leaned towards me again and touched my arm with polished fingertips:

"I'll tell you what I would like, and that's a sandwich." She wrinkled her nose in an anxious way. "Would it cost so much more than a drink?"

"A sandwich won't break me. Let's go."

On the way to the diner, every man on the train looked at her ankles. She ordered a turkey sandwich, all white meat please, and drummed on the tablecloth until it arrived. It disappeared in no time. She was ravenous.

"Have another," I said.

"Do you think I should?" She gave me a dubious look. Not calculating exactly, just questioning.

"You seem to be pretty hungry."

"I am. But."

"No personal obligation. I like to see hungry people eat."

"You're awfully kind. And I am awfully hungry. But. Are you sure you can afford it?"

"Money is no object. I just collected a thousand-dollar fee. If you can use a full-course dinner, say so."

"Oh no. I couldn't possibly accept *that*. But I would like another sandwich, since you're so very kind."

I signalled to the waiter. The second sandwich went the way of the first.

"Feeling better now? You were looking a little peaked."

"Much better. I'm ashamed to admit it, but I hadn't eaten all day. And I've been on short rations for a week."

I looked her over, deliberately. Her dark blue suit was new, and expensively cut. Her bag was fine calfskin. She wore a wafer-thin wristwatch made of white gold. If she was broke, she was putting up a good front.

"I know what you're thinking," she said. "I could have pawned something. Only I couldn't *bear* to. I spent my last cent on my ticket, and I thought I could hold out until I got to Los Angeles. I would have, too, if it hadn't been for you. You broke me down with kindness."

"Forget it about my kindness. I hope you have a job waiting for you. Or maybe a husband?"

"Neither of those things. You have one more guess."

She giggled like a schoolgirl, and it gave me an idea:

"You flunked out of school."

"Not exactly. I'm still enrolled at Berkeley. You're very acute, aren't you? Did you say you're a lawyer?"

"What gave you that idea?"

"You mentioned a fee you earned. A thousand-dollar fee. That sounds like a lawyer to me."

"I'm a private detective," I said. "My name is Lew Archer."

Her reaction was disconcerting. She gripped the edge of the table with her hands, and pushed herself away from it. Her eyes darkened to a turbulent purple. She said in a voice as thin and sharp as a razor:

"Did Edward hire you? To spy on me?"

"Of course," I said conversationally. "That's why I told you I'm a detective. I'm very sly. And who in hell is Edward?"

"Edward Illman. Are you sure he didn't employ you to pick — to contact me? Cross your heart?"

The colored waiter edged towards our table, attracted by the urgent note in her voice. "Something the matter, lady?"

"No, thank you."

She managed to give him a strained smile, and he went away with many backward looks.

"Oh sure," I said. "Why certainly. Edward employed me to feed you poisoned sandwiches. Don't you feel your feet turning cold? You can expect the other symptoms in a little while. Cheyne-Stokes breathing and all."

"Please. You mustn't joke about such things. I wouldn't put it past him. After what he did to Ethel."

"And who is Ethel?"

"My sister, my older sister. She's a darling. But Edward doesn't think so. He hates us both. I wouldn't be surprised if he's responsible for all this."

I said: "This is getting us nowhere. Obviously you're in some kind of a jam. You want to tell me about it and I want to hear about it. Now take a few deep breaths and start over, from the beginning. Bear in mind that I don't know these people from Adam. I don't even know your name."

"I'm sorry. My name is Clare Larrabee."

Dutifully, she inhaled. Her snub-nosed breasts rose under her blouse, and she made a very pretty picture, three-dimensional. The third dimension was the prettiest.

"I've been talking like a silly fool, haven't I? I'm worried about Ethel, though. I haven't heard from her for several weeks. I don't know where she is or what's happened to her. Last week when my allowance didn't come, I started to get really worried. I phoned her house in West Hollywood and got no answer. Since then I've been phoning several times a day, with never an answer. So finally I swallowed my pride and got in touch with Edward. He said he hasn't seen her since she went to

Nevada for her divorce. Of course I don't necessarily believe him. He's a notorious liar. You should have heard him when they arranged the settlement, perjuring himself right and left."

"Edward keeps cropping up," I said. "Let's get it straight about Edward. Is he your sister Ethel's husband?"

"He was. Ethel divorced him last month. And she's well rid of him, even if he did cheat her out of her fair share. He claimed to be nearly broke, but I know better. He's a big real estate operator, practically a millionaire. You must have heard of the Illman Tract in the Valley."

"This is the same Illman?"

"Yes. Do you know him?"

"I've seen his name in the columns. He's quite a Casanova, isn't he?"

"He's a terrible man." Her mouth pounted out in girlish indignation. "He even had the gall to make a — make advances to me, when Ethel was still married to him. I told him what I thought of him, don't worry."

"And now you're thinking he had something to do with your sister's disappearance?"

"I'm sure of it. He sounded so smug when I phoned him long distance yesterday from Berkeley. I tell you, Edward is capable of anything. If something's happened to Ethel, I know who's responsible."

"She's probably all right," I said, "off on a little trip or something."

"You don't know Ethel. She'd never dream of going away and leaving me stranded at school without any money. I held out as long as I could, hoping to hear from her. When I got down to my last twenty dollars, I decided to take the train home."

"To Ethel's house in West Hollywood?"

"Yes. It's the only home I have since Daddy passed away. Ethel's the only family I have. I couldn't bear to lose her." Her blue eyes filmed with tears.

"Do you have taxi-fare?"

She shook her head, shamefaced.

"I'll drive you out. I don't live far from there myself. My car's stashed in a garage near the station."

"You're being good to me." Her hand crept out across the tablecloth and pressed the back of mine. "Forgive me for saying those silly things, about Edward hiring you."

"Skip it."

2.

We drove out Sunset and up into the hills. Afternoon was changing imperceptibly into evening. The horizontal sunlight flashed like blinding searchlights from the western windows of the hillside apartment buildings. Clare huddled anxiously in the far corner of the seat. She didn't speak, except to direct me to her sister's house.

It was a flat-roofed building set high on a sloping lot. The walls were redwood and glass, and the redwood had not yet weathered grey. I parked on the slanting blacktop drive and got out. Both stalls of the carport under the house were empty. The drapes were pulled over the giant windows that overlooked the valley.

I knocked on the front door. The noise resounded emptily through the building. I tried it. It was locked. So was the service door at the side.

I turned to the girl at my elbow. She was clutching the handle of her overnight bag with both hands, and looking pinched again. I thought that it was a cold homecoming for her.

"Nobody home," I said.

"It's what I was afraid of. What shall I do now?"

"You share this residence with your sister?"

"When I'm home from school."

"And it belongs to her?"

"Since the divorce it does."

"Then you can give me permission to break in."

"All right. But please don't damage anything if you can help it. Ethel is very proud of her house."

The side door had a spring-type lock. I took a rectangle of plastic out of my wallet, and slipped it into the crack between the door and the frame. The lock slid back easily.

"You're quite a burglar," she said in a dismal attempt at humor.

I stepped inside without answering her. The kitchen was bright and clean, but it had a slightly musty, disused odor. The bread in the breadbox was stale. The refrigerator needed defrosting. There was a piece of ham mouldering on one shelf, and on another a half-empty bottle of milk which had gone sour.

"She's been gone for some time," I said. "At least a week. We should check her clothes."

"Why?"

"She'd take some along if she left to go on a trip, under her own power."

"I see."

She led me through the living room, which was simply and expensively furnished in black iron and net, into the master bedroom. The huge square bed was neatly made, and covered with a pink quilted silk spread. Clare looked away from it, as if the conjunction of a man and a bed gave her a guilty feeling. While she went through the closet, I searched the vanity and the chest of drawers.

They were barer than they should have been. Cosmetics were conspicuous by their absence. I found one thing of interest in the top drawer of the vanity, hidden under a tangle of stockings: a bank book issued by the Las Vegas branch of the Bank of Southern California. Ethel Illman had deposited thirty thousand dollars on March 14 of this year. On March 17 she had withdrawn five thousand dollars. On March 20 she had withdrawn six thousand dollars. On March 22 she had withdrawn eighteen thousand, nine hundred and ninety-five dollars. There was a balance in her account, after service charges, of $3.65.

Clare said from the closet in a muffled voice:

"A lot of her things are gone. Her mink stole, her good suits and shoes, a lot of her best summer clothes."

"Then she's probably on a vacation." I tried to keep the doubt out of my voice. A woman wandering around the southwest with thirty thousand dollars in cash was taking a big chance. I decided not to worry Clare with that, and put the little bank book in my pocket.

"Without telling me? Ethel wouldn't do that." She came out of the closet, pushing her fine light hair back from her forehead. "You don't understand how close we are to each other, closer than sisters usually are. Ever since father died —"

"Does she drive her own car?"

"Of course. It's a last year's Buick convertible, robin's-egg blue."

"If you're badly worried, go to Missing Persons."

"No. Ethel wouldn't like that. She's a very proud person, and shy. Anyway, I have a better idea." She gave me that questioning-calculating look of hers.

"Involving me?"

"Please." Her eyes in the darkening room were like great soft centerless pansies, purple or black. "You're a detective, and evidently a good one. And you're a man. You can stand up to Edward and make him answer questions. He just laughs at me. I can't pay you in advance —"

"Forget the money for now. What makes you so certain that Illman is in on this?"

"I just know he is. He threatened her in the lawyer's office the day they made the settlement. She told me so herself. Edward said that he was going to get that money back if he had to take it out of her hide. He wasn't fooling, either. He's beaten her more than once."

"How much was the settlement?"

"Thirty thousand dollars and the house and the car. She could have collected much more, hundreds of thousands, if she'd stayed in California and fought it through the courts. But she was too anxious to get free from him. So she let him cheat her, and got a Nevada divorce instead. And even then he wasn't satisfied."

She looked around the abandoned bedroom, fighting back tears. Her skin was so pale that it seemed to be phosphorescent in the gloom. With a little cry, she flung herself face down on the bed and gave herself over to grief. I said to her shaking back:

"You win. Where do I find him?"

3.

He lived in a pueblo hotel on the outskirts of Bel-Air. The gates of the walled pueblo were standing open, and I went in. A few couples were strolling on the gravel paths among the palm-shaded cottages, walking off the effects of the cocktail hour or working up an appetite for dinner. The women were blonde, and had money on their backs. The men were noticeably older than the women, except for one, who was noticeably younger. They paid no attention to me.

I passed an oval swimming pool, and found Edward Illman's cottage, number twelve. Light streamed from its open french windows onto a flagstone terrace. A young woman in a narrow-waisted, billowing black gown lay on a chrome chaise at the edge of the light. With her arms hanging loose from her naked shoulders, she looked like an expensive French doll which somebody had accidentally dropped there. Her face was polished and plucked and painted, expressionless as a doll's. But her eyes snapped open at the sound of my footsteps.

"Who goes there?" she said with a slight Martini accent. "Halt and give the password or I'll shoot you dead with my atomic wonder-weapon." She pointed a wavering finger at me and said: "Bing. Am I supposed to know you? I have a terrible memory for faces."

"I have a terrible face for memories. Is Mr. Illman home?"

"Uh-huh. He's in the shower. He's always taking showers. I told him he's got a scour-and-scrub neurosis, his mother was frightened by a washing machine." Her laughter rang like cracked bells. "If it's about business, you can tell me."

"Are you his confidential secretary?"

"I was." She sat up on the chaise, looked pleased with herself. "I'm his fiancée, at the moment."

"Congratulations."

"Uh-huh. He's loaded." Smiling to herself, she got to her feet. "Are you loaded?"

"Not so it gets in my way."

She pointed her finger at me and said bing and laughed again, teetering on her four-inch heels. She started to fall forward on her face. I caught her under the armpits.

"Too bad," she said to my chest. "I don't think you have a terrible face for memories at all. You're much prettier than old Teddybear."

"Thanks. I'll treasure the compliment."

I set her down on the chaise, but her arms twined round my neck like smooth white snakes and her mouth opened over mine, a fleshy red sea anemone. She clung to me like a drowning child. I had to use force to detach myself.

"What's the matter?" she said, pointing. "You a fairy?"

A man appeared in the french windows, blotting out most of the light. In a white terry-cloth bathrobe, he had the shape and bulk of a Kodiak bear. Eyes like wet brown stones gleamed in the crannies of his face. The top of his head was as bald as an ostrich egg. He carried a chip on each shoulder, like epaulets.

"What goes on?"

"Your fiancée swooned, slightly."

"Fiancée hell. I saw what happened." Moving very quickly and lightly for a man of his age and weight, he pounced on the girl in the chaise and began to shake her. "Can't you keep your hands off anything in pants?"

Her head bobbed back and forth. Her teeth clicked like castanets.

I put a rough hand on his shoulder. "Leave her be."

He turned on me. "Who do you think you're talking to?"

"Edward Illman, I presume."

"And who are you?"

"The name is Archer. I'm looking into the matter of your wife's disappearance."

"I'm not married. And I have no intention of getting married. I've been burned once." He looked down sideways at the girl. She gazed up at him in silence, taut with fear and hatred.

"Your ex-wife, then," I said.

"Has something happened to Ethel?"

"I thought you might be able to tell me."

"Where did you get that idea? Have you been talking to Clare?"

I nodded.

"Don't believe her. She's got a down on me, just like her sister. Because I had the misfortune to marry Ethel, they both think I'm fair game for anything they want to pull. I wouldn't touch either one of them with an insulated pole. They're a couple of hustlers, if you want the truth. They took me for sixty grand and what did I get out of it but headaches?"

"I thought it was thirty."

"Sixty," he said, with the money light in his eyes. "Thirty in cash, and the house is worth another thirty, easily."

I looked around the place, which must have cost him fifty dollars a day. Above the palms, the first few stars sparkled like solitaire diamonds.

"You seem to have some left."

"Sure I have. But I work for my money. Ethel was strictly from nothing when I met her. She owned the clothes on her back and what was under them and that was all. So she gives me a bad time for three years and I pay off at the rate of twenty grand a year. I ask you, is that fair?"

"I hear you threatened to get it back from her."

"You *have* been talking to Clare, huh? All right, so I threatened her. It didn't mean a thing. I talk too much sometimes, and I have a bad temper."

"I'd never have guessed."

The girl said: "You hurt me, Teddy. I need another drink. Get me another drink, Teddy."

"Get it yourself."

She called him several bad names and wandered into the cottage, walking awkwardly like an animated doll.

He grasped my arm. "What's the trouble about Ethel? You said she disappeared. You think something's happened to her?"

I shook his hand off. "She's missing. Thirty thousand in cash is also missing. There are creeps in this town who would knock her off for one big bill, or less."

"Didn't she bank the money? She wouldn't cash a draft for that amount and carry it around. She's crazy, but not that way."

"She banked it all right, on March 14. Then she drew it all out again in the course of the following week. When did you send her the draft?"

"The twelfth or the thirteenth. That was the agreement. She got her final divorce on March 11."

"And you haven't seen her since?"

"I have not. Frieda has, though."

"Frieda?"

"My secretary." He jerked a thumb towards the cottage. "Frieda went over to the house last week to pick up some of my clothes I'd left behind. Ethel was there, and she was all right then. Apparently she's taken up with another man."

"Do you know his name?"

"No, and I couldn't care less."

"Do you have a picture of Ethel?"

"I did have. I tore them up. She's a well-stacked blonde. She looks very much like Clare, same coloring, but three or four years older. You should be able to get a picture from Clare. And while you're at it, tell her for me she's got a lot of gall setting the police on me. I'm a respectable businessman in this town." He puffed out his chest under the bathrobe. It was thickly matted with brown hair, beginning to grizzle.

"No doubt," I said. "Incidentally, I'm not the police. I run a private agency. My name is Archer."

"So that's how it is." The planes of his broad face gleamed angrily in the light. He cocked a fat red fist. "You come here pumping me. Get out, by God, or I'll throw you out."

"Calm down. I could break you in half."

His face swelled with blood, and his eyes popped. He swung a roundhouse right at my head. I stepped inside of it and tied him up. "I said calm down, mister. You'll break a vein."

I pushed him off balance and released him. He sat down very suddenly in the chaise. Frieda was watching us from the edge of the terrace. She laughed so heartily that she spilled her drink.

Illman looked old and tired, and he was breathing raucously through his mouth. He didn't try to get up. Frieda came over to me and leaned her weight on my arm. I could feel her small sharp breasts.

"Why didn't you hit him," she whispered, "when you had the chance? He's always hitting other people." Her voice rose. "Teddy-bear thinks he can get away with murder."

"Shut your yap," he said, "or I'll shut it for you."

"Button yours, muscleman. You'll lay a hand on me once too often."

"You're fired."

"I already quit."

They were a charming couple. I was on the point of tearing myself away when a bellboy appeared from nowhere, like a gnome in uniform:

"A gentleman to see you, Mr. Illman."

The gentleman was a brown-faced young Highway Patrolman, who stepped forward rather diffidently into the light. "Sorry to trouble you, sir. Our San Diego office asked me to contact you as soon as possible."

Frieda looked from me to him, and began to gravitate in his direction. Illman got up heavily and stepped between them:

"What is it?"

The patrolman unfolded a teletype flimsy and held it up to the light. "Are you the owner of a blue Buick convertible, last year's model?" He read off the license number.

"It was mine," Illman said. "It belongs to my ex-wife now. Did she forget to change the registration?"

"Evidently she did, Mr. Illman. In fact, she seems to've forgotten the car entirely. She left it in a parking space above the public beach in La Jolla. It's been sitting there for the last week, until we hauled it in. Where can I get in touch with Mrs. Illman?"

"I don't know. I haven't seen her for some time."

The patrolman's face lengthened and turned grim. "You mean she's dropped out of sight?"

"Out of my sight, at least. Why?"

"I hate to have to say this, Mr. Illman. There's a considerable quantity of blood on the front seat of the Buick, according to this report. They haven't determined yet if it's human blood, but it looks like murder."

"Good heavens! It's what we've been afraid of, isn't it, Archer?" His voice was as thick as corn syrup with phony emotionalism. "You and Clare were right after all."

"Right about what, Mr. Illman?" The patrolman looked slightly puzzled.

"About poor Ethel," he said. "I've been discussing her disappearance with Mr. Archer here. Mr. Archer is a private detective, and I was just about to engage his services to make a search for Ethel." He turned to me with a painful smile pulling his mouth to one side. "How much did you say you wanted in advance? Five hundred?"

"Make it two. That will buy my services for four days. It doesn't buy anything else, though."

"I understand that, Mr. Archer. I'm sincerely interested in finding Ethel for a variety of reasons, as you know."

He was a suave old fox. I almost laughed in his face. But I played along with him. I liked the idea of using his money to hang him, if possible.

"Yeah. This is a tragic occurrence for you."

He took a silver money clip shaped like a dollar sign out of his bathrobe pocket. I wondered if he didn't trust his roommate. Two centuries changed hands. After a further exchange of information, the patrolman went away.

"Well," Illman said. "This looks like a pretty serious business. If you think I had anything to do with it, you're off your rocker."

"You talk too much." I turned to Frieda, who looked as if the news had sobered her. "Who was this fellow you saw at Ethel's house last week?"

"I dunno. She called him Owen, I think. Maybe it was his first name, maybe it was his last name. She didn't introduce us." She said it as if she felt cheated.

"Describe him?"

"Sure. A big guy, over six feet, wide in the shoulders, narrow in the beam. A smooth hunk of male. And young," with a malicious glance at Illman. "Black hair and he had all of his hair, dreamy dark eyes, a cute little hairline moustache. I tabbed him for a gin-mill cowboy from L. V., but he could be a movie star if I was a producer."

"Thank God you're not," Illman said.

"What made you think she'd taken up with him?"

"The way he moved around the house, like he owned it. He poured himself a drink while I was there. And he was in his shirtsleeves. A real sharp dresser, though. Custom-made stuff."

"You have a good eye."

"For me, she has," Illman said.

"Lay off me," she said in a hard voice, with no trace of the Martini drawl. "Or I'll really walk out on you and then where will you be?"

"Right where I am now. Sitting pretty."

"That's what you think."

I interrupted their communion: "Do you know anything about this Owen character, Illman?"

"Not me. He's probably some jerk she picked up in Nevada while she was sweating out the divorce."

"Have you been to San Diego recently?"

"Not for months."

"That's true," Frieda said. "I've been keeping close track of Teddy. I have to. Incidentally, it's getting late and I'm hungry. Go and put on some clothes, darling. You're prettier with clothes on."

"More than I'd say for you," he leered.

4.

I left them and drove back to West Hollywood. The night-blooming girls and their escorts had begun to appear on the Strip. Gusts of music came from the doors that opened for them. But when I turned off Sunset, the streets were deserted, emptied by the television curfew.

All the lights were on in the redwood house on the hillside. I parked in the driveway and knocked on the front door. The drapes over the window beside it were pulled to one side, then fell back into place. A thin voice drifted out to me:

"Is that you, Mr. Archer?"

I said that it was. Clare opened the door inch by inch. Her face was almost haggard:

"I'm so relieved to see you."

"What's the trouble?"

"A man was watching the house. He was sitting there at the curb in a long black car. It looked like an undertaker's car. And it had a Nevada license."

"Are you sure?"

"Yes. It lighted up when he drove away. I saw it through the window. He only left a couple of minutes ago."

"Did you get a look at his face?"

"I'm afraid not. I didn't dare go out. I was petrified. He shone a searchlight on the window."

"Take it easy. There are plenty of big black cars in town, and quite a few Nevada licenses. He was probably looking for some other address."

"No. I had a — a kind of a fatal feeling when I saw him. I just *know* that he's connected in some way with Ethel's disappearance. I'm scared."

She leaned against the door, breathing quickly. She looked very young and vulnerable. I said:

"What am I going to do with you, kid? I can't leave you here alone."

"Are you going away?"

"I have to. I saw Edward. While I was there, he had a visitor from the HP. They found your sister's car abandoned near San Diego." I didn't mention the blood. She had enough on her mind.

"Edward killed her!" she cried. "I knew it."

"That I doubt. She may not even be dead. I'm going to San Diego to find out."

"Take me along, won't you?"

"It wouldn't be good for your reputation. Besides, you'd be in the way."

"No, I wouldn't. I promise. I have friends in San Diego. Just let me drive down there with you, and I can stay with them."

"You wouldn't be making this up?"

"Honest, I have friends there. Gretchen Falk and her husband, they're good friends of Ethel's and mine. We lived in San Diego for a while, before she married Edward. The Falks will be glad to let me stay with them."

"Hadn't you better phone them first?"

"I can't. The phone's disconnected. I tried it."

"Are you sure these people exist?"

"Of course," she said urgently.

I gave in. I turned out the lights and locked the door and put her unpacked bag in my car. Clare stayed very close to me.

As I was backing out, a car pulled in behind me, blocking the entrance to the driveway. I opened the door and got out. It was a black Lincoln with a searchlight mounted over the windshield.

Clare said: "He's come back."

The searchlight flashed on. Its bright beam swivelled towards me. I reached for the gun in my shoulder holster and got a firm grip on nothing. Holster and gun were packed in the suitcase in the trunk of my car. The searchlight blinded me.

A black gun emerged from the dazzle, towing a hand and an arm. They belonged to a quick-stepping cube-shaped man in a double-breasted flannel suit. A snap-brim hat was pulled down over his eyes. His mouth was as full of teeth as a barracuda's. It said:

"Where's Dewar?"

"Never heard of him."

"Owen Dewar. You've heard of him."

The gun dragged him forward another step and collided with my breastbone. His free hand palmed my flanks. All I could see was his unchanging smile, framed in brilliant light. I felt a keen desire to do some orthodontal work on it. But the gun was an inhibiting factor.

"You must be thinking of two other parties," I said.

"No dice. This is the house, and that's the broad. Out of the car, lady."

"I will not," she said in a tiny voice behind me.

"Out, or I'll blow a hole in your boyfriend here."

Reluctantly, she clambered out. The teeth looked down at her ankles as if they wanted to chew them. I made a move for the gun. It dove into my solar plexus, doubling me over. Its muzzle flicked the side of my head. It pushed me back against the fender of my car. I felt a worm of blood crawling past my ear.

"You coward! Leave him alone." Clare flung herself at him. He sidestepped neatly, moving on the steady pivot of the gun against my chest. She went to her knees on the blacktop.

"Get up, lady, but keep your voice down. How many boyfriends you keep on the string, anyway?"

She got to her feet. "He isn't my boyfriend. Who are you? Where is Ethel?"

"That's a hot one." The smile intensified. "You're Ethel. The question is, where's Dewar?"

"I don't know any Dewar."

"Sure you do, Ethel. You know him well enough to marry him. Now tell me where he is, and nobody gets theirselves hurt." The flat voice dropped, and added huskily: "I haven't got much time to waste."

"You're wrong," she said. "You're completely mistaken. I'm not Ethel. I'm Clare. Ethel's my older sister."

He stepped back and swung the gun in a quarter-circle, covering us both. "Turn your face to the light. Let's have a good look at you."

She did as she was told, striking a rigid pose. He shifted the gun to his left hand, and brought a photograph out of his inside pocket. Looking from it to her face, he shook his head doubtfully:

"I guess you're levelling at that. You're younger than this one, and thinner." He handed her the photograph. "She your sister?"

"Yes. It's Ethel."

I caught a glimpse of the picture over her shoulder. It was a blownup candid shot of two people. One was a pretty blonde who looked like Clare five years from now. She was leaning on the arm of a tall dark man with a hairline moustache. They were smirking at each other, and there was a flower-decked altar in the background.

"Who's the man?" I said.

"Dewar. Who else?" said the teeth behind the gun. "They got married in L. V. last month. I got this picture from the Chaparral Chapel. It goes with the twenty-five dollar wedding." He snatched it out of Clare's hands and put it back in his pocket. "It took me a couple of weeks to run her down. She used her maiden name, see?"

"Where did you catch up with her? San Diego?"

"I didn't catch up with her. Would I be here if I did?"

"What do you want her for?"

"I don't want her. I got nothing against the broad, except that she tied up with Dewar. He's the boy I want."

"What for?"

"You wouldn't be inarested. He worked for me at one time." The gun nodded at Clare. "You know where your sister is?"

"No, I don't. I wouldn't tell you if I did."

"That's no way to talk now, lady. My motto's cooperation. From other people."

I said: "Her sister's been missing for a week. The HP found her car in San Diego. It had bloodstains on the front seat. Are you sure you didn't catch up with her?"

"I'm asking the questions, punk." But there was a trace of uncertainty in his voice.

"What happened to Dewar if the blonde is missing?"

"I think he ran out with her money."

Clare turned to me: "You didn't tell me all this."

"I'm telling you now."

The teeth said: "She had money?"

"Plenty."

"The bastard. The bastard took us both, huh?"

"Dewar took you for money?"

"You ask too many questions, punk. You'll talk yourself to death one of these days. Now stay where you are for ten minutes, both of you. Don't move, don't yell, don't telephone. I might decide to drive around the block and come back and make sure."

He backed down the brilliant alley of the searchlight beam. The door of his car slammed. All of its lights went off together. It rolled away into darkness, and didn't come back.

5.

It was past midnight when we got to San Diego, but there was still a light in the Falks' house. It was a stucco cottage on a street of identical cottages in Pacific Beach.

"We lived here once," Clare said. "When I was going to high school. That house second from the corner." Her voice was nostalgic, and she looked around the jerry-built tract as if it represented something precious to her. The pre-Illman era in her young life.

I knocked on the Falks' front door. A big henna-head in a house-coat opened it on a chain. But when she saw Clare beside me, she flung the door wide:

"Clare honey, where you been? I've been trying to phone you in Berkeley, and here you are. How are you, honey?"

She opened her arms and the younger woman walked into them.

"Oh, Gretchen," she said with her face on the redhead's breast. "Something's happened to Ethel, something terrible."

"I know it, honey, but it could be worse."

"Worse than murder?"

"She isn't murdered. Put that out of your mind. She's pretty badly hurt, but she isn't murdered."

Clare stood back to look at her face. "You've seen her? Is she here?"

The redhead put a finger to her mouth, which was big and generous looking like the rest of her. "Sh, Clare. Jake's asleep, he has to get up early, go to work. Yeah, I've seen her, but she isn't here. She's in a nursing home over on the other side of town."

"You said she's badly hurt?"

"Pretty badly beaten, yeah, poor dear. But the doctor told me she's pulling out of it fine. A little plastic surgery, and she'll be as good as new."

"Plastic surgery?"

"Yeah, I'm afraid she'll need it. I got a look at her face tonight, when they changed the bandages — Now take it easy, honey. It could be worse."

"Who did it to her?"

"That lousy husband of hers."

"Edward?"

"Heck, no. The other one. The one that calls himself Dewar, Owen Dewar."

I said: "Have you seen Dewar?"

"I saw him a week ago, the night he beat her up, the dirty rotten bully." Her deep contralto growled in her throat. "I'd like to get my hands on him just for five minutes."

"So would a lot of people, Mrs. Falk."

She glanced inquiringly at Clare. "Who's your friend? You haven't introduced us."

"I'm sorry. Mr. Archer, Mrs. Falk. Mr. Archer is a detective, Gretchen."

"I was wondering. Ethel didn't want me to call the police. I told her she ought to, but she said no.

The poor darling's so ashamed of herself, getting mixed up with that kind of a louse. She didn't even get in touch with *me* until tonight. Then she saw in the paper about her car being picked up, and she thought maybe I could get it back for her without any publicity. Publicity is what she doesn't want most. I guess it's a tragic thing for a beautiful girl like Ethel to lose her looks."

"I'm a private detective," I said. "There won't be any publicity if I can help it. Did you go to see the police about her car?"

"Jake advised me not to. He said it would blow the whole thing wide open. And the doctor told me he was kind of breaking the law by not reporting the beating she took. So I dropped it."

"How did this thing happen?"

"I'll tell you all I know about it. Come on into the living room, kids, let me fix you something to drink."

Clare said: "You're awfully kind, Gretchen, but I must go to Ethel. Where is she?"

"The Mission Rest Home. Only don't you think you better wait till morning? It's a private hospital, but it's awful late for visitors."

"I've got to see her," Clare said. "I couldn't sleep a wink if I didn't. I've been so worried about her."

Gretchen heaved a sigh. "Whatever you say, honey. We can try, anyway. Give me a second to put on a dress and I'll show you where the place is."

She led us into the darkened living room, turned the television set off and the lights on. A quart of beer, nearly full, stood on a coffee-table beside the scuffed davenport. She offered me a glass, which I accepted gratefully. Clare refused. She was so tense she couldn't even sit down.

We stood and looked at each other for a minute. Then Gretchen came back, struggling with a zipper on one massive hip.

"All set. You better drive, Mr. Archer. I had a couple of quarts to settle my nerves. You wouldn't believe it, but I've gained five pounds since Ethel came down here. I always gain weight when I'm anxious."

We went out to my car, and turned towards the banked lights of San Diego. The women rode in the front seat. Gretchen's opulent flesh was warm against me.

"Was Ethel here before it happened?" I said.

"Sure she was, for a day. Ethel turned up here eight or nine days ago, Tuesday of last week it was. I hadn't heard from her for several months, since she wrote me that she was going to Nevada for a divorce. It was early in the morning when she drove up, in fact she got me out of bed. The minute I saw her, I knew that something was wrong. The poor kid was scared, really scared. She was as cold as a corpse, and her teeth were chattering. So I fed her some coffee and put her in a hot tub, and after that she told me what it was that'd got her down."

"Dewar?"

"You said it, mister. Ethel never was much of a picker. When she was hostessing at the Grant coffee shop back in the old days, she was always falling for the world's worst phonies. Speaking of phonies, this Dewar takes the cake. She met him in L. V. when she was waiting for her divorce from Illman. He was a big promoter, to hear him tell it. She fell for the phony story, and she fell for him. A few days after she got her final decree, she married him. Big romance. Big deal. They were going to be business partners, too. He said he had some money to invest, twenty-five thousand or so, and he knew of a swell little hotel in Acapulco that they could buy at a steal for fifty thousand. The idea was that they should each put up half, and go and live in Mexico in the lap of luxury for the rest of their lives. He didn't show her any of his money, but she believed him. She drew her settlement money out of the bank and came to L. A. with him to close up her house and get set for the Mexican deal."

"He must have hypnotized her," Clare said. "Ethel's a smart business woman."

"Not with something tall, dark and handsome, honey. I give him that much. He's got the looks. Well, they lived in L. A. for a couple of weeks, on Ethel's money of course, and he kept putting off the Mexican trip. He didn't want to go anywhere, in fact, just sit around the house and drink her liquor and eat her good cooking."

"He was hiding out," I said.

"From what? The police?"

"Worse than that. Some gangster pal from Nevada was gunning for him, still is. Ethel wasn't the only one he fleeced."

"Nice guy, eh? Anyway, Ethel started to get restless. She didn't like sitting around with all that money in the house, waiting for nothing. Last Monday night, a week ago Monday that is, she had a showdown with him. Then it all came out. He didn't have any money or anything else. He wasn't a promoter, he didn't know of any hotel in Acapulco. His whole build-up was as queer as a three-dollar bill. Apparently he made his living gambling, but he was even all washed up with that. Nothing. But she was married to him now, he said, and she was going to sit still and like it or he'd knock her block off.

"He meant it, too, Ethel said. She's got the proof of it now. She waited until he drank himself to sleep that night, then she threw some things in a bag, including her twenty-five thousand, and came down here. She was on her way to get a quickie divorce in Mexico, but Jake and me talked her into staying for a while and thinking it over. Jake said she could probably get an annulment right in California, and that would be more legal."

"He was probably right."

"Yeah? Maybe it wasn't such a bright idea after all. We kept her here just long enough for Dewar to catch her. Apparently she left some letters behind, and he ran down the list of her friends until he found her at our place. He talked her into going for a drive to talk it over. I didn't hear what was said — they were in her room — but he must have used some powerful persuasion. She went out of the house with him as meek as a lamb, and they drove away in her car. That was the last I saw of her, until she got in touch with me tonight. When she didn't come back, I wanted to call the police, but Jake wouldn't let me. He said I had no business coming between a man and his wife and all that guff. I gave Jake a piece of my mind tonight on that score. I ought to've called the cops as soon as Dewar showed his sneaking face on our front porch."

"What exactly did he do to her?"

"He gave her a bad clobbering, that's obvious. Ethel didn't want to talk about it much tonight. The subject was painful to her in more ways than one."

"Did he take her money?"

"He must have. It's gone. So is he."

We were on the freeway which curved past the hills of Balboa Park. The trees of its man-made jungle were restless against the sky. Below us on the other side, the city sloped like a frozen cascade of lights down to the black concavity of the bay.

The Mission Rest Home was in the eastern suburbs, an old California-Spanish mansion which had been converted into a private hospital. The windows in its thick stucco walls were small and barred, and there were lights in some of them.

I rang the doorbell. Clare was so close to my back I could feel her breath. A woman in a purple flannelette wrapper opened the door. Her hair hung in two grey braids, which were ruler-straight. Her hard black eyes surveyed the three of us, and stayed on Gretchen.

"What is it now, Mrs. Falk?" she said brusquely.

"This is Mrs. — Miss Larrabee's sister Clare."

"Miss Larrabee is probably sleeping. She shouldn't be disturbed."

"I know it's late," Clare said in a tremulous voice. "But I've come all the way from San Francisco to see her."

"She's doing well, I assure you of that. She's completely out of danger."

"Can't I just go in for a teensy visit? Ethel will want to see me, and Mr. Archer has some questions to ask her. Mr. Archer is a private detective."

"This is very irregular." Reluctantly, she opened the door. "Wait here, and I'll see if she is awake. Please keep your voices down. We have other patients."

We waited in a dim high-ceilinged chamber which had once been the reception room of the mansion. The odors of mustiness and medication blended depressingly in the stagnant air.

"I wonder what brought her here," I said.

"She knew old lady Lestina," Gretchen said. "She stayed with her at one time, when Mrs. Lestina was running a boarding-house."

"Of course," Clare said. "I remember the name. That was when Ethel was going to San Diego State. Then Daddy — got killed, and she had to drop out of school and go to work." Tears glimmered in her eyes. "Poor Ethel. She's always tried so hard, and been so good to me."

Gretchen patted her shoulder. "You bet she has, honey. Now you have a chance to be good to her."

"Oh, I will. I'll do everything I can."

Mrs. Lestina appeared in the arched doorway. "She's not asleep. I guess you can talk to her for a very few minutes."

We followed her to a room at the end of one wing of the house. A white-uniformed nurse was waiting at the door. "Don't say anything to upset her, will you? She's always fighting sedation as it is."

The room was large but poorly furnished, with a mirrorless bureau, a couple of rickety chairs, a brown-enameled hospital bed. The head on the raised pillow was swathed in bandages through which tufts of blonde hair were visible. The woman sat up and spread her arms. The whites of her eyes were red, suffused with blood from broken vessels. Her swollen lips opened and said, "Clare!" in a tone of incredulous joy.

The sisters hugged each other, with tears and laughter. "It's wonderful to see you," the older one said through broken teeth. "How did you get here so fast?"

"I came to stay with Gretchen. Why didn't you call me, Ethel? I've been worried sick about you."

"I'm dreadfully sorry, darling. I should have, shouldn't I? I didn't want you to see me like this. And I've been so ashamed of myself. I've been such a terrible fool. I've lost our money."

The nurse was standing against the door, torn between her duty and her feelings. "Now you promised not to get excited, Miss Larrabee."

"She's right," Clare said. "Don't give it a second thought. I'm going to leave school and get a job and look after you. You need some looking after for a change."

"Nuts. I'll be fine in a couple of weeks." The brave voice issuing from the mask was deep and vibrant. "Don't make any rash decisions, kiddo. The head is bloody but unbowed." The sisters looked at each other in the silence of deep affection.

I stepped forward to the bedside and introduced myself. "How did this happen to you, Miss Larrabee?"

"It's a long story," she lisped, "and a sordid one."

"Mrs. Falk has told me most of it up to the point when Dewar made you drive away with him. Where did he take you?"

"To the beach, I think it was in La Jolla. It was late and there was nobody there and the tide was coming in. And Owen had a gun. I was terrified. I didn't know what more he wanted. He already had my twenty-five thousand."

"He had the money?"

"Yes. It was in my room at Gretchen's house. He made me give it to him before we left there. But it didn't satisfy him. He said I hurt his pride by leaving him. He said he had to satisfy his pride." Contempt ran through her voice like a thin steel thread.

"By beating you up?"

"Apparently. He hit me again and again. I think he left me for dead. When I came to, the waves were splashing on me. I managed somehow to get up to the car. It wasn't any good to me, though, because Owen had the keys. It's funny he didn't take it."

"Too easily traced," I said. "What did you do then?"

"I hardly know. I think I sat in the car for a while, wondering what to do. Then a taxi went by and I stopped him and told him to bring me here."

"You weren't very wise not to call the police. They might have got your money back. Now it's a cold trail."

"Did you come here to lecture me?"

"I'm sorry. I didn't mean —"

"I was half-crazy with pain," she said. "I hardly knew what I was doing. I couldn't bear to have anybody see me."

Her fingers were active among the folds of the sheets. Clare reached out and stroked her hands into quietness. "Now, now darling," she crooned. "Nobody's criticizing you. You take things nice and easy for a while, and Clare will look after you."

The masked head rolled on the pillow. The nurse came forward, her face solicitous. "I think Miss Larrabee's had enough, don't you?"

She showed us out. Clare lingered with her sister for a moment, then followed us to the car. She sat between us in brooding silence all the way to Pacific Beach. Before I dropped them off at Gretchen's house, I asked for her permission to go to the police. She wouldn't give it to me, and nothing I could say would change her mind.

6.

I spent the rest of the night in a motor court, trying to crawl over the threshold of sleep. Shortly after dawn I disentangled myself from the twisted sheets and drove out to La Jolla. La Jolla is a semi-detached suburb of San Diego, a small resort town half-surrounded by sea. It was a grey morning. The slanting streets were scoured with the sea's cold breath, and the sea itself looked like hammered pewter.

I warmed myself with a short-order breakfast and went the rounds of the hotels and motels. No one resembling Dewar had registered in the past week. I tried the bus and taxi companies, in vain. Dewar had slipped out of town unnoticed. But I did get a lead on the taxi-driver who had taken Ethel to the Mission Rest Home. He had mentioned the injured woman to his dispatcher, and the dispatcher gave me his name and address. Stanley Simpson, 38 Calle Laureles.

Simpson was a paunchy, defeated-looking man who hadn't shaved for a couple of days. He came to the door of his tiny bungalow in his underwear, rubbing sleep out of his eyes. "What's the pitch, bub? If you got me up to try and sell me something, you're in for a disappointment."

I told him who I was and why I was there. "Do you remember the woman?"

"I hope to tell you I do. She was bleeding like a stuck pig, all over the back seat. It took me a couple of hours to clean it off. Somebody pistol-whipped her, if you ask me. I wanted to take her to the hospital, but she said no. Hell, I couldn't argue with her in that condition. Did I do wrong?" His slack mouth twisted sideways in a self-doubting grimace.

"If you did, it doesn't matter. She's being taken good care of. I thought you might have got a glimpse of the man that did it to her."

"Not me, mister. She was all by herself, nobody else in sight. She got out of a parked car and staggered out into the road. I couldn't just leave her there, could I?"

"Of course not. You're a good Samaritan, Simpson. Exactly where did you pick her up?"

"Down by the Cove. She was sitting in this Buick. I dropped a party off at the beach club and I was on my way back, kind of cruising along —"

"What time?"

"Around ten o'clock, I guess it was. I can check my schedule."

"It isn't important. Incidentally, did she pay you for the ride?"

"Yeah, she had a buck and some change in her purse. She had a hard time making it. No tip," he added gloomily.

"Tough cheese."

His fogged eyes brightened. "You're a friend of hers, aren't you? Wouldn't you say I rate a tip on a run like that? I always say, better late than never."

"Is that what you always say?" I handed him a dollar.

The Cove was a roughly semicircular inlet at the foot of a steep hill, surmounted by a couple of hotels. Its narrow curving beach and the street above it were both deserted. An offshore wind had swept away the early-morning mist, but the sky was still cloudy, and the sea grim. The long swells slammed the beach like stone walls falling, and broke in foam on the rocks that framed the entrance to the Cove.

I sat in my car and watched them. I was at a dead end. This seaswept place, under this iron sky, was like the world's dead end. Far out at sea, a carrier floated like a chip on the horizon. A Navy jet took off from it and scrawled tremendous nothings on the distance.

Something bright caught my eye. It was in the trough of a wave a couple of hundred yards outside the Cove. Then it was on a crest: the aluminum air-bottle of an Aqualung strapped to a naked brown back. Its wearer was prone on a surfboard, kicking with black-finned feet towards the shore. He was kicking hard, and paddling with one arm, but he was making slow progress. His other arm dragged in the opaque water. He seemed to be towing something, something heavy. I wondered if he had speared a shark or a porpoise. His face was inscrutable behind its glass mask.

I left my car and climbed down to the beach. The man on the surfboard came towards me with his tiring one-armed stroke, climbing the walled waves and sliding down them. A final surge picked him up and set him on the sand, almost at my feet. I dragged his board out of the backwash, and helped him to pull in the line that he was holding in one hand. His catch was nothing native to the sea. It was a man.

The end of the line was looped around his body under the armpits. He lay face down like an exhausted runner, a big man, fully clothed in soggy tweeds. I turned him over and saw the aquiline profile, the hairline moustache over the blue mouth, the dark eyes clogged with sand. Owen Dewar had made his escape by water.

The skin-diver took off his mask and sat down heavily, his chest working like a great furred bellows. "I go down for abalone," he said between breaths. "I find this. Caught between two rocks at thirty–forty feet."

"How long has he been in the water?"

"It's hard to tell. I'd say a couple of days, anyway. Look at his color. Poor stiff. But I wish they wouldn't drown themselves in my hunting-grounds."

"Do you know him?"

"Nope. Do you?"

"Never saw him before," I said, with truth.

"How's about you phoning the police, Mac? I'm pooped. And unless I make a catch, I don't eat today. There's no pay in fishing for corpses."

"In a minute."

I went through the dead man's pockets. There was a set of car-keys in his jacket pocket, and an alligator wallet on his hip. It contained no money, but the driver's license was decipherable: Owen Dewar, Mesa Court, Las Vegas. I put the wallet back, and let go of the body. The head rolled sideways. I saw the small round hole in the neck, washed clean by the sea.

"Holy Mother," the diver said. "He was shot."

7.

I got back to the Falk house around mid-morning. The sun had burned off the clouds, and the day was turning hot. The long, treeless street of identical houses looked cheap and rundown by daylight. It was part of the miles of suburban slums that the war had scattered all over Southern California.

Gretchen was sprinkling the brown front lawn with a desultory hose. She looked too big for the pocket-handkerchief yard. The sunsuit that barely covered her various bulges made her look even bigger. She turned off the water when I got out of my car.

"What gives? You've got trouble on your face if I ever saw trouble."

"Dewar is dead. Murdered. A skin-diver found him in the sea off La Jolla."

She took it calmly. "That's not such bad news, is it? He had it coming. Who killed him?"

"I told you a gunman from Nevada was on his trail. Maybe he caught him. Anyway, Dewar was shot and bled to death from a neck wound. Then he was dumped in the ocean. I had to lay the whole thing on the line for the police, since there's murder in it."

"You told them what happened to Ethel?"

"I had to. They're at the rest home talking to her now."

"What about Ethel's money? Was the money on him?"

"Not a trace of it. And he didn't live to spend it. The police pathologist thinks he's been dead for a week. Whoever got Dewar got the money at the same time."

"Will she ever get it back, do you think?"

"If we can catch the murderer, and he still has it with him. That's a big if. Where's Clare, by the way? With her sister?"

"Clare went back to L. A."

"What for?"

"Don't ask me." She shrugged her rosy shoulders. "She got Jake to drive her down to the station before he went to work. I wasn't up. She didn't even tell me she was going." Gretchen seemed peeved.

"Did she get a telegram, or a phone call?"

"Nothing. All I know is what Jake told me. She talked him into lending her ten bucks. I wouldn't mind so much, but it was all the ready cash we had, until payday. Oh well, I guess we'll get it back, if Ethel recovers her money."

"You'll get it back," I said. "Clare seems to be a straight kid."

"That's what I always used to think. When they lived here, before Ethel met Illman and got into the chips, Clare was just about the nicest kid on the block. In spite of all the trouble in her family."

"What trouble was that?"

"Her father shot himself. Didn't you know? They said it was an accident, but the people on the street — we knew different. Mr. Larrabee was never the same after his wife left him. He spent his time brooding, drinking and brooding. Clare reminded me of him, the way she behaved last night after you left. She wouldn't talk to me or look at me. She shut herself up in her room and acted real cold. If you want the honest truth, I don't like her using my home like it was a motel and Jake was a taxi-service. The least she could of done was say goodbye to me."

"It sounds as if she had something on her mind."

All the way back to Los Angeles, I wondered what it was. It took me a little over two hours to drive from San Diego to West Hollywood. The black Lincoln with the searchlight and the Nevada license plates was standing at the curb below the redwood house. The front door of the house was standing open.

I transferred my automatic from the suitcase to my jacket pocket, making sure that it was ready to fire. I climbed the terraced lawn beside the driveway. My feet made no sound in the grass. When I reached the porch, I heard voices from inside. One was the gunman's hoarse and deathly monotone:

"I'm taking it, sister. It belongs to me."

"You're a liar."

"Sure, but not about this. The money is mine."

"It's my sister's money. What right have you got to it?"

"This. Dewar stole it from me. He ran a poker game for me in L. V., a high-stakes game in various hotels around town. He was a good dealer, and I trusted him with the house take. I let it pile up for a week, that was my mistake. I should've kept a closer watch on him. He ran out on me with twenty-five grand or more. That's the money you're holding, lady."

"I don't believe it. You can't prove that story. It's fantastic."

"I don't have to prove it. I'm the one with the gun. Gelt talks, but iron talks louder. So hand it over."

"I'll die first."

"Maybe you will at that," he said blandly.

I edged along the wall to the open door. Clare was standing flat against the opposite wall of the hallway. She was clutching a sheaf of bills to her breast. The gunman's broad flannel back was to me, and he was advancing on her.

"Stay away from me, you." Her cry was thin and desperate. She was trying to merge with the wall, her body agonized by an orgiastic terror.

"I don't like taking candy from a baby," he said in a very reasonable tone. "Only I'm going to have that money back."

"You can't have it. It's Ethel's. It's all she has."

"— you, lady. You and your sister both."

He raised his armed right hand and slapped the side of her face with the gun-barrel, lightly. Fingering the welt it left, she said in a kind of despairing stupor:

"You're the one that hurt Ethel, aren't you? Now you're hurting me. You like hurting people."

"Listen to reason, lady. It ain't just the money, it's a matter of business. I let it happen once, it'll happen again. I can't afford to let nobody get away with nothing. I got a reputation to live up to.

I said from the doorway: "Is that why you killed Dewar?"

He let out an animal sound, and whirled in my direction. I shot before he did, twice. The first slug rocked him back on his heels. His bullet went wild, ploughed the ceiling. My second slug took him off balance and slammed him against the wall. His blood splattered Clare and the money in her hands. She screamed once, very loudly.

The man from Las Vegas dropped his gun. It clattered on the parquetry. His hands pressed his perforated chest, trying to hold the blood in. He slid down the wall slowly, his face a mask of smiling pain, and sat with a bump on the floor. He blew red bubbles and said:

"You got me wrong. I didn't kill Dewar. I didn't know he was dead. The money belongs to me. You made a big mistake, punk."

"So did you."

He went on smiling, as if in fierce appreciation of the joke. Then his red grin changed to a rictus, and he slumped sideways.

Clare looked from him to me, her eyes wide and dark with the sight of death. "I don't know how to thank you. He was going to kill me."

"I doubt that. He was just combining a little pleasure with business."

"But he shot at you."

"It's just as well he did. It leaves no doubt that it was self-defense."

"Is it true what you said? That Dewar's dead? He killed him?"

"You tell me."

"What do you mean?"

"You've got the money that Dewar took from your sister. Where did you get it?"

"It was here, right in this house. I found it in the kitchen."

"That's kind of hard to swallow, Clare."

"It's true." She looked down

at the blood-spattered money in her hands. The outside bill was a hundred. Unconsciously, she tried to wipe it clean on the front of her dress. "He had it hidden here. He must have come back and hid it."

"Show me where."

"You're not being very nice to me. And I'm not feeling well."

"Neither is Dewar. You didn't shoot him yourself, by any chance?"

"How could I? I was in Berkeley when it happened. I wish I was back there now."

"You know when it happened, do you?"

"No." She bit her lip. "I don't mean that. I mean I was in Berkeley all along. You're a witness, you were with me on the train coming down."

"Trains run both ways."

She regarded me with loathing. "You're not nice at all. To think that yesterday I thought you were nice."

"You're wasting time, Clare. I have to call the police. But first I want to see where you found the money. Or where you say you did."

"In the kitchen. You've got to believe me. It took me a long time to get here from the station on the bus. I'd only just found it when he walked in on me."

"I'll believe the physical evidence, if any."

To my surprise, the physical evidence was there. A red-enameled flour canister was standing open on the board beside the kitchen sink. There were fingermarks in the flour, and a floury piece of oilskin wrapping in the sink.

"He hid the money under the flour," Clare said. "I guess he thought it would be safer here than if he carried it around with him."

It wasn't a likely story. On the other hand, the criminal mind was capable of strange things. Whose criminal mind, I wondered: Clare's, or Owen Dewar's, or somebody else's? I said:

"Where did you get the bright idea of coming back here and looking for it?"

"Ethel suggested it last night, just before I left her. She told me this was his favorite hiding-place while she was living with him. She discovered it by accident one day."

"Hiding-place for what?"

"Some kind of drug he took. He was a drug-addict. Do you still think I'm lying?"

"Somebody is. But I suppose I've got to take your word, until I get something better. What are you going to do with the money?"

"Ethel said if I found it, that I was to go down and put it in the bank."

"There's no time for that now. You better let me hold it for you. I have a safe in my office."

"No. You don't trust me. Why should I trust you?"

"Because you can trust me, and you know it. If the cops impound it, you'll have to prove ownership to get it back."

She was too spent to argue. She let me take it out of her hands. I riffled through the bills and got a rough idea of their sum. There was easily twenty-five thousand there. I gave her a receipt for that amount, and put the sheaf of bills in my inside pocket.

8.

It was after dark when the cops got through with me. By that time I was equipped to do a comparative study on the San Diego and Los Angeles P.D.'s. With the help of a friend in the D.A.'s office, Clare's eye-witness account, and the bullet in the ceiling, I got away from them without being booked. The dead man's record also helped. He had been widely suspected of shooting Bugsy Siegel, and had fallen heir to some of Siegel's holdings. His name was Jack Fidaris. R.I.P.

I drove out Sunset to my office. The Strip was lighting up for business again. The stars looked down on its neon conflagration like hard bright knowing eyes. I pulled the venetian blinds and locked the doors and counted the money: twenty-six thousand, three hundred and eighty dollars. I wrapped it up in brown paper, sealed it with wax and tucked it away in the safe. I would have preferred to tear it 'n little pieces and flush the green confetti down the drain. Two men had died for it. I wasn't eager to become the third.

I had a steak in the restaurant at International Airport, and hopped a shuttle plane to Las Vegas. There I spent a rough night in various gambling joints, watching the suckers blow their vacation money, pinching my own pennies, and talking to some of the guys and girls that raked the money in. The rest of Illman's two hundred dollars bought me the facts I needed.

I flew back to Los Angeles in the morning, picked up my car and headed for San Diego. I was tired enough to sleep standing up like a horse. But something heavier than sleep or tiredness sat on the back of my neck and pressed the gas-pedal down to the floorboards. It was the thought of Clare.

Clare was with her sister at the Mission Rest Home. She was waiting outside the closed door of Ethel's room when Mrs. Lestina took me down the hall. She looked as if she had passed a rougher night than mine. Her grooming was careless, hair uncombed, mouth unpainted. The welt from Fidaris' gun had turned blue and spread to one puffed eye. And It hought how very little it took to break a young girl down into a tramp, if she was vulnerable, or twist her into something worse than a tramp.

"Did you bring it with you?" she said as soon as La Lestina was out of earshot. "Ethel's very angry with me for turning it over to you."

"I'm not surprised."

"Give it to me. Please." Her hand clawed at my sleeve. "Isn't that what you came for, to give it back to me?"

"It's in the safe in my office in Los Angeles. That is, if you're talking about the money."

"What else would I be talking about? You'll simply have to go back there and get it. Ethel can't leave here without it. She needs it to pay her bill."

"Is Ethel planning to go someplace?"

"I persuaded her to come back to Berkeley with me. She'll have better care in the hospital there, and I know of a good plastic surgeon —"

"It'll take more than that to put Ethel together again."

"What do you mean?"

"You should be able to guess. You're not a stupid girl, or are you? Has she got you fooled the way she had me fooled?"

"I don't know what you're talking about. But I don't like it. Every time I see you, you seem to get nastier."

"This is a nasty business. It's rubbing off on all of us, isn't it, kid?"

She looked at me vaguely through a fog of doubt. "Don't you dare call me kid. I thought you were a real friend for a while, but you don't even like me. You've said some dreadful things. You probably think you can scare me into letting you keep our money. Well, you can't."

"That's my problem," I said. "What to do with the money."

"You'll give it back to Ethel and me, that's what you'll do. There are laws to deal with people like you —"

"And people like Ethel. I want to talk to her."

"I won't let you. My sister's suffered enough already."

She spread her arms across the width of the door, in the attitude of crucifixion. I was tempted to go away and send her the money and forget the whole thing. All I had for Clare was longer and sharper nails. But the need to finish it pushed me, imperative as a gun at my back.

I lifted her by the waist and tried to set her aside. Her entire body was rigid and jerking galvanically. Her hands slid under my arms and around my back and held on. Her head rolled on my shoulder and was still. Suddenly, like delayed rain after lightning, her tears came. I stood and held her vibrating body, trying to quench the dangerous heat that was rising in my veins, and wondering what in hell I was going to do.

"Ethel did it for me," she sobbed. "She wanted me to have a good start in life."

"Some start she's giving you. Did she tell you that?"

"She didn't have to. I knew. I tried to pretend to myself, but I knew. When she told me where to look for the money that night."

"You knew that Ethel took it from Dewar and hid it in her house?"

"Yes. The thought went through my mind, and I couldn't get rid of it. Ethel's always taken terrible chances, and money means so much to her. Not for herself. For me."

"She wasn't thinking of you when she gambled away the money she got from Illman. She went through it in a week."

"Is that what happened to it?"

"That's it. I flew to Las Vegas last night and talked to some of the people that got her money, dealers and croupiers. They remembered her. She had a bad case of gambling fever that week. It didn't leave her until the money was gone. Then maybe she thought of you."

"Poor Ethel. I've seen her before when she had a gambling streak."

"Poor Dewar," I said. "He was the goat."

The door beside us creaked open. The empty eye of a blue revolver looked out. Above it, Ethel's eyes glared red from her bandaged face.

"Come in here, both of you."

Clare stretched out her hands towards her sister. "No, Ethel. Darling, you mustn't. Give me that gun."

"I have a use for it. I know what I'm doing."

She backed away, supporting herself on the doorknob.

I said to Clare: "We better do as she says. She won't hurt you."

"Nor you unless you make me. Don't reach for your gun, and don't try anything funny. You know what happened to Dewar."

"Not as well as you do."

"Don't waste any tears on that one. Save them for yourself. Now get in here." The gun wagged peremptorily.

I edged past her with Clare at my back. Ethel shut the door and moved to the bed, her eyes never leaving mine. She sat on its edge, and supported the elbow of her gun arm on her knee, hunched far over like an aged wreck of a woman.

It was strange to see the fine naked legs dangling below her hospital gown, the red polish flaking off her toenails. Her voice was low and resonant:

"I don't like to do this. But how am I going to make you see it my way if I don't? I want Clare to see it, too. It was self-defense, understand? I didn't intend to kill him. I never expected to see him again. Fidaris was after him, and it was only a matter of time until he caught up with Owen. Owen knew that. He told me himself he wouldn't live out the year. He was so sure of it that he was paralyzed. He got so he wouldn't even go out of the house.

"Somebody had to make a move, and I decided it might as well be me. Why should I sit and wait for Fidaris to come and take the money back and blow Owen's head off for him? It was really my money, anyway, mine and Clare's."

"Leave me out of this," Clare said.

"But you don't understand, honey," the damaged mouth insisted. "It really was my money. We were legally married, what was his was mine. I talked him into taking it in the first place. He'd never have had the guts to do it alone. He thought Fidaris was God himself. I didn't. But I didn't want to be there when Jack Fidaris found him. So I left him. I took the money out of his pillow when he was asleep and hid it where he'd never look for it. Then I drove down here. I guess you know the rest. He found a letter from Gretchen in the house, and traced me through it. He thought I was carrying the money. When it turned out that I wasn't, he took me out to the beach and beat me up. I wouldn't tell him where it was. He threatened to shoot me then. I fought him for the gun, and it went off. It was a clear case of self-defense."

"Maybe it was. You'll never get a jury to believe it, though. Innocent people don't dump their shooting victims in the drink."

"But I didn't. The tide was coming in. I didn't even touch him after he died. He just lay there, and the water took him."

"While you stood and watched?"

"I couldn't get away. I was so weak I couldn't move for a long time. Then when I finally could, it was too late. He was gone, and he had the keys to the car."

"He drove you out to La Jolla?"

"Yes."

"And held a gun on you at the same time. That's quite a trick."

"He did, though," she said. "That is the way it happened."

"I hear you telling me, Mrs. Dewar."

She winced behind her mask at the sound of her name. "I'm not Mrs. Dewar," she said. "I've taken back my maiden name. I'm Ethel Larrabee."

"We won't argue about the name. You'll be trading it in for a number, anyway."

"The hell I will. The shooting was self-defense, and once he was dead the money belonged to me. There's no way of proving he stole it, now that Fidaris is gone. I guess I owe you a little thanks for that."

"Put down your gun, then."

"I'm not that grateful," she said.

Clare moved across the room towards her. "Let me look at the gun, Ethel. It's father's revolver, isn't it?"

"Be quiet, you little fool."

"I won't be quiet. These things have to be said. You're way off by yourself, Ethel, I'm not with you. I want no part of this, or the money. You don't understand how strange and dreadful —" Her voice broke, momentarily. She stood a few feet from her sister, held back by the gun's menace, yet strongly drawn towards it. "That's father's revolver, isn't it? The one he shot himself with?"

"What if it is?"

"I'll tell you, Ethel," I said. "Dewar didn't pull a gun on you. You were the one that had the gun. You forced him to drive you out to the beach and shot him in cold blood. But he didn't die right away. He lived long enough to leave his marks on you. Isn't that how it happened?"

The bandaged face was silent. I looked into the terrible eyes for assent. They were lost and wild, like an animal's. "Is that true, Ethel? Did you murder him?" Clare looked down at her sister with pity and loathing.

"I did it for you," the masked face said. "I always tried to do what was best for you. Don't you believe me? Don't you know I love you? Ever since father killed himself I've tried —"

Clare turned and walked to the wall and stood with her forehead against it.

Ethel put the muzzle of the gun in her mouth. Her broken teeth clenched on it the way a smoker bites on a pipestem. The bone and flesh muffled its roar.

I laid her body out on the bed and pulled a sheet up over it.

The Bobby-Soxer

The man appeared from nowhere and caught her. There was no escape.

BY
JONATHAN
CRAIG

It was almost ten o'clock on a sultry August night when Donna Taylor turned the corner at Howard Street and started walking west toward Center Avenue. She was seventeen, but without make-up and dressed as she was now, in white blouse and plaid skirt and saddle shoes, she could have passed for a year or so younger than that.

She was a remarkably pretty girl, with slim tapering legs that were tanned to almost the same dark-gold color of the hair caught at the nape of her neck in a pony tail, but she seemed completely unaware of the appreciative glances following her.

She was humming to herself as she walked. Just before she reached the avenue, she paused to look at the display in a store window. A tall, middle-aged man in a pin-striped suit was looking at the display, too. When he saw Donna, he kept his face toward the window, but his eyes stayed on her. They were funny eyes, shifty and sort of wild.

She hesitated a moment, then moved around him, walking in the direction of the avenue again.

Just as she reached the mouth of the alley beside the store building, she heard a quick step behind her. A hand went over her mouth, and a man's arm whipped around her body in such a way that her arms were pinioned to her sides. She felt herself being lifted off her feet, and then she was being dragged into the blackness of the alley.

She struggled against him, but it was useless. The man carried her as easily as if she had been a doll.

When he had taken her a dozen yards into the alley, he stopped and forced her down to the pavement.

Terror sickened through her. And then she felt the man's sweaty palm across her mouth slip a half inch to one side, and she jerked her head violently in the other direction. For just an instant her mouth was uncovered, and she screamed. She knew, instinctively, that the man would be afraid after it was over and would try to kill her, and she screamed so loudly that her ears rang.

The man cursed and jumped to his feet, and his heels echoed hollowly on the pavement as he ran toward the mouth of the alley.

Then, out in the street, she heard the pounding of other feet, and men yelling, and she got up and steadied herself against the wall. Then she began to walk toward the mouth of the alley, very slowly, trying to catch her breath.

She came out on the street just as two shirt-sleeved men started into the alley.

"You all right?" one of the men asked.

She nodded. Across the street she caught sight of the man in the pin-striped suit. He was being held by three other men, one of whom had grabbed his hair and jerked his head back. He was trying to fight his way loose, but a man had hold of each of his arms, and they were standing slightly in back of him so that he couldn't kick at them.

One of the men in shirt-sleeves put his arm around Donna and led her over to the man who had attacked her. She looked at him, and then looked down at the sidewalk.

The other shirt-sleeved man said, "Exactly what happened, Miss — not that I can't guess."

Donna didn't look up. "He pulled me into the alley," she said. "He — tried to . . ." Her voice trailed off.

"For God's sake, Ed!" one of the men said. "Aren't you bright enough to know what happened, without making her talk about it?" He stepped close to the man in the pin-striped suit and hit him flush in the mouth. "You son of a bitch," he said softly.

Donna glanced about her. A crowd was forming now. She didn't know any of the men and women who were pressing in close. The man in shirt-sleeves still had his arm around her, gently and protectively, the way her father sometimes held her. She heard the newcomers asking questions, and the indignant, angry replies they made when they learned what had happened.

She looked at the man in the pin-striped suit again. There was blood at the corner of his mouth and his eyes were sick with fear.

A woman stepped up to him and shook her fist in his face. "You ought to hang!" she said. "A little girl like that! Why, she's hardly more than a baby!" She spat in the man's face.

"Anybody call the cops?" someone asked.

"Joe's just run back to his candy store to call," someone else said.

The man in the pin-striped suit made a sudden, violent lunge and broke free from the men who had been holding him. He stumbled and went to one knee, then righted himself and started to run. A foot went out to trip him, and he sprawled headlong on the cement. Before he could get up again, a man in a flowered sport shirt leaped upon him and pulled his arm up behind his back in a hammerlock.

Another man drew back his foot and kicked the fallen man in the ribs. The attacker screamed, but the foot sank into his ribs again and again.

The woman who had spit at him said, "That's the way, George! Kick him in the face!"

Donna turned away. She felt as if she might be sick at her stomach.

The man who had his arm around her said, "You poor little kid . . ." Then the man on the ground screamed again, and Donna heard the meaty impact of a shoe-toe meeting his face.

"Kick his damn head off, George!" the woman yelled.

"You better stop," someone said. "You'll kill him if you aren't careful."

A police siren keened on the heavy night air, rising and falling, coming fast.

The police cruiser turned the corner and squealed to a stop. The crowd moved back, and suddenly there was no sound other than the sobbing moans of the man on the sidewalk. He was lying on his back now, motionless, his face battered to a swollen, bleeding pulp. One wrist had been broken, and two inches of bone shard had pushed through the skin.

Fifteen minutes later, Donna sat on a wooden bench at the station house, talking to Sergeant Clinton. The police had taken her attacker to a hospital under guard.

"You sure you wouldn't rather we took you home in a squad car?" Clinton asked.

She shook her head. "My folks, they would . . ."

"All right, then," Clinton said gently. "But make sure you bring them right back here with you. We got to get your statement, and we got to have your folks here on account of you're a minor."

Donna turned and walked slowly out of the station house and along the street until she reached the corner. Then she quickened her pace, and another five minutes brought her to Center Avenue, the main drag along which she walked every evening, and for which she had been heading when she had paused to look in the store window. She was still shaken from her experience, but rapidly beginning to return to normal.

Half a block farther on, she stopped before another store window. And at this window too a man was looking at the display. He was about the same age and size as her attacker had been, but *he* looked all right, not funny and wild-eyed like the other one, This man, she knew, would be okay.

She glanced both ways along the avenue, and then she said softly, "You want to have a party, mister?"

The man looked at her, first with surprise and then with interest.

"What would it cost me?" he asked.

She smiled at him. "A fiver," she said.

MUGGED AND PRINTED

MICKEY SPILLANE, author of the world-wide best-sellers *I, The Jury* — recently released as a 3-D Technicolor film — *My Gun Is Quick, Vengeance Is Mine* and many others — was accorded a startling honor a few months back, when the American Booksellers' Association issued statistics on the best-selling books of the year 1952. First: the Bible. Second: Mickey Spillane. His latest book, *Kiss Me, Deadly,* is now smashing all records. *The Girl Behind The Hedge,* in this issue, is top-drawer Spillane — which is reason enough to read it immediately.

JOHN ROSS MACDONALD, *Manhunt's* most mysterious contributor, is back in this issue with a new Lew Archer novelette, *The Beat-Up Sister.* The guesses on his identity (still pouring in!) range from the flat statement that MacDonald is Raymond Chandler to the confusing theory we received from one anonymous reader that MacDonald's stories are dictated by spirits, and "written by no human hand." All agree, though, that MacDonald is one of the best writers in the mystery field — as *The Beat-Up Sister* proves.

DAVID GOODIS has a hobby of being put in jail. When he comes to New York, he likes to drag out his old clothes, which make him, he says, "look like a rather well-dressed bum," and wander through the city's slum areas, gathering background for novels like the famous *Cassidy's Woman, Dark Passage, Nightfall* and others. He has often been picked up by patrolmen who notice that he's just a little too well-dressed for the neighborhood — and sometimes it's several days before he can convince them he's a writer and not a mobster. Marking the whole thing down to research, he leaves the station-house, goes back to his Philadelphia home, and turns out more authentic, quietly terrifying yarns like *Professional Man,* in this issue.

RICHARD S. PRATHER, author of six novels for Gold Medal, including *Bodies In Bedlam, Everybody Had A Gun* and his latest, *Darling, It's Death,* which is climbing to the top of the sales charts, has had a small variety of jobs, including four years in the Merchant Marine ("duties consisting largely of walking around with a greasy rag in my pocket"), three years as a Civil Service clerk, and hours of spare time as a sonneteer. But he's never been either a professional gangster or a private eye — which leaves us wondering just where he got the authentic background for his tough and fast-moving *Squeeze Play* in this issue, featuring private peeper Shell Scott, together with several professional mobsters.

FLOYD MAHANNAH is preoccupied with colors, to judge by his novels *The Golden Goose* and *The Yellow Hearse.* This time, it's green — as in his latest story, *Where's The Money?* • SAM S. TAYLOR somehow found time to turn out the terrific and startling *Summer Is A Bad Time* for *Manhunt,* in spite of the fact that he's got a new novel (*So Cold, My Bed*) coming out in October, and a reprint of his *No Head For Her Pillow* in September. • ROBERT TURNER (*Dead Heat*) has worked all three sides of the literary triangle, as agent, editor and writer. Now he's sticking purely to writing — "it makes less ulcers," he claims. • VINCENT H. GADDIS collects factual crimes — like those in this month's *Crime Cavalcade* — while his wife, Margaret Gaddis, concocts fictional ones for Crime Club

CAPTAIN FUTURE
WIZARD OF SCIENCE
COMET
FICTION AND FACT OF THE PRIZE-RING
FIGHT STORIES
THE BLACK UHLAN
HEADQUARTERS DETECTIVE
MASKED RIDER WESTERN
FIGHTING ACES OF WAR SKIES
WINGS
10 STORY WESTERN MAGAZINE
ADVENTURE NOVELS
Thrilling Stories of the Sky Trails
Air STORIES
THE NIGHT HAWK
FIGHTING DAREDEVILS OF TODAY'S WAR
AIR WAR
THE ALL-STORY
WARLORD of MARS
ARMY Romances
BASKETBALL STORIES
Battle Stories
O'LEARY IN ACTION IN ETHIOPIA
BLACK BOOK DETECTIVE
GOLDEN FLEECE
HIGH-SEAS ADVENTURES
INDIAN Stories
BRIDE OF THE TOMAHAWK PACK
MY LIFE WITH SITTING BULL
LONE RANGER
MAGIC CARPET MAGAZINE
PEARLS FROM MACAO
MARVEL SCIENCE STORIES
NEW DETECTIVE
North-West ROMANCES
GIRLS OF WHITE WATER TRAIL
Oriental STORIES
PHANTOM DETECTIVE
PLANET STORIES
QUEEN OF THE MARTIAN CATACOMBS
POPULAR DETECTIVE
PRIVATE DETECTIVE
LOVE STORIES OF THE REAL WEST
RANCH ROMANCES
Maid of the Valley
RANGE RIDERS
SIX-GUN VALLEY
Vice Squad DETECTIVE
SECRET of the HOUSE of HORROR
TOP-NOTCH STORIES ... TOP-NOTCH WRITERS
UNDERWORLD DETECTIVE
THRILLING WONDER STORIES
THE FEDERALS IN ACTION
G-MEN
SCIENCE FICTION
SPICY-ADVENTURE STORIES
HELL'S RIVER

www.ingramcontent.com/pod-product-compliance
Lightning Source LLC
LaVergne TN
LVHW090959080826
845145LV00003B/1056

* 9 7 8 1 6 4 7 2 0 6 7 1 0 *